THE WITCH'S HEART

Book One of the One Part Witch Series

IRIS KINCAID

THE WITCH'S HEART
Copyright 2017 by Iris Kincaid

Cover design by Kerri Knutson
Editing by Valorie Clifton
ISBN - 13: 978-154-7227044
ISBN: - 10: 1547227044

CHAPTER ONE

Witches aren't invincible. And despite their legendary longevity, nor are they immortal. That said, there was no earthly reason for Lilith Hazelwood, the most powerful witch in Oyster Cove, to meet her doom at the tender age of ninety-two. Her natural lifespan should have guaranteed another thirty years.

Admittedly, Lilith had been struck by a bolt of lightning. And to the naïve eye, she simply seemed like the random victim of cruel chance. The coroner would later rule it to be an accident, and why not? Why couldn't it simply be an accident, or bad luck?

Because accidents and bad luck were things that Lilith Hazelwood created for others. Someone being capable of sending Lilith to her grave was so inconceivable, it had never even crossed her mind. It's a very humbling thing to know that someone has defeated you. All right, maybe not so much humbling as enraging. Humility was not really an emotion in Lilith's wheelhouse.

Like most creatures at the top of the food chain, she feared no one. It would be easier to sneak up on a grizzly bear than to get within striking range of Lilith. The breadth of her innate talent was unfathomable, the full range of her mastery of all witchcraft powers unmatched in her corner of the world.

She could read minds, manipulate emotions, transform matter, converse with the dead, compel the unwilling to bend to her whim, and generally wreak havoc to her heart's content. Her supremacy was well-known among the local witches, and no one dared challenge it. All members of the local witch population had considerable strengths, but no one came close to Lilith's staggering range of abilities.

And she never hesitated to use those talents. She flexed her power for much the same reason that bodybuilders flex their muscles—because she could. She was also quite happy for others to witness her supremacy, including humans. Most of the witches in Oyster Cove preferred to live under the radar. But a small handful wanted to be acknowledged and feared.

There was good reason to fear Lilith. She was one of the small number of local witches who regularly engaged in the dark arts, meaning that every few years or so, someone met their demise at her hands. There was nothing capricious about it. She only killed people who had offended her moral code—yes, even Lilith Hazelwood had a moral code—child molesters, wife beaters, and murderers. She had done Oyster Cove a service in getting rid of people who were a public menace, a blight on society. In fact, so many evildoers in Oyster Cove had died under mysterious circumstances that the local saying had arisen, "Anyone who dies in Oyster Cove deserves it."

She was unappointed and all-powerful judge, jury, and executioner. Some might have argued that Lilith herself could be classified as a menace. Not to her face. She was understandably blind to her own misconduct and keenly aware of that of others. In that way, she was more humanly flawed than she would ever have acknowledged.

No wonder, then, that she was barely cognizant of the moment of her own demise. Yes, she did sense that she had entered an otherworldly realm, but it was not the first time that Lilith's spirit had parted from her body. It was a high-level ability that she had practiced on countless occasions. Her previous excursions into the astral plane had involved witnessing her own lovely and youthful body slumbering peacefully below. But her body did not look peaceful—it was decidedly lifeless and charred!

The shock of being dead was all but overshadowed by Lilith's rage at the immediate understanding that she'd been the target of foul play. Someone had actually gotten the best of her. Who? Why? And most importantly, by what means was she going to get her vengeance?

*****

Dr. Harold Svenson was not an unkind or ghoulish man. But he had to admit, if only to himself, how excited he was at the prospect of a fresh dead body. He was a transplant specialist, after all. He had a multitude of patients in debilitating or life or death situations awaiting suitable organs for transplant. But his excitement was clouded by a long moment of paralyzed uncertainty upon hearing the name of the dead victim—Lilith Hazelwood.

Dr. Svenson was born and raised in Oyster Cove. He'd left for some thirty-odd years for medical school and a long and distinguished career in Boston. He returned to the lively artsy tourist town some five years ago, determined to cut his workload in half but still fiercely committed to his remaining patients. Lilith's name and face were very familiar to him. He had known of her when he was a child, and she was a hypnotic and mysterious older woman. Now that he had become a frequent patron of the local theater's classic movie nights, he would most aptly describe Lilith as a ringer for Ava Gardner. She was about twenty years his senior, as near as he could figure.

But the corpse that lay before him, and indeed, the woman herself whom he'd seen from a distance around town these past few years since his return, was no older than forty years of age. Closer to late thirties, in fact. In other words, a woman who had once been twenty years his senior was now more than twenty years his junior. The passage of time had added a headful of white hair and a moderately lined brow to his own appearance, but Lilith Hazelwood had seemed downright resistant to the concept of aging. He hadn't really been aware of whether she was a witch before he left Oyster Cove, but now that he was back, there was little doubt.

Equally telling was the fact that when her body was received, the assault from the lightning bolt had left her skin burned and smoldering. Now, some four hours later, although she was indisputably dead, her skin had undergone a remarkable repair. Not unlike human hair and nails that continue to grow after death, some regenerative force was still at work in her otherwise lifeless body. His mind started spinning at the transplant possibilities.

His twenty-three-year-old assistant, Ruby Townsend, raced into the exam room.

"Is she a donor?" she asked breathlessly.

The doctor took a deep breath. "Indeed she is, Ruby. She's the perfect donor."

"So we need a copy of her license. Or did she sign the donor thing? Has her family signed off on this? And you've probably checked the donor registries already. Do any of our patients have priority? Oh please, please, please tell me that we're going to get something."

"We're going to get everything, Ruby. Heart, lungs, corneas, thyroid, brain, skin graft, eardrums, windpipe, thyroid, bone marrow . . . I'm going to drain her of every drop of blood. Everything, you hear me? Everything! And there's no donor registry to consult. Not with this body. Not with this donor."

Ruby looked as if she was about to hyperventilate. She sank into the nearest chair. "What do you mean no registry? That's what we always do. That's what we have to do. By law."

The doctor knelt in front of her. He needed to look her in the eyes and he also needed to plead. "Listen to me very carefully, Ruby. This woman is a witch. You know about the witches in Oyster Cove, yes?"

Ruby nodded with wide, frightened eyes. "That Fiona Skretting is a witch. At least that's what I've heard. And there are more. But it's just so hard to tell. Most of the witches are older, aren't they? This woman is really, really young. What makes you so sure that she is a witch?"

"Because she was an adult when I was a child. She has to be in her early nineties at the youngest. And look at these photographs that I took of her wounds from when she arrived three hours ago. And look at the skin now. There's something highly regenerative about her body. I don't know anything for certain, but this could be the miracle I've been praying for."

"But . . . the hospital won't allow it. We don't have the papers. We don't have permission."

The doctor put his hands gently on top of Ruby's "We don't have papers. But I tell you what we do have. We have at least half a dozen patients who have a chance to be saved from miserable disability and even death. You know Margo Bailey? I've known her for ten years. She's a sweet girl, so resigned to the fact that she won't have a future. None of the happiness and security that I have known in my own life. None of the wondrous anticipation that should lie before every young person. I have spent many a night thinking of Margo Bailey and wondering what I would do if I ever obtained a heart that would save her life and there was no donor permission. What would I do? What would I be *willing* to do to give that girl a future? Would I break the law? Falsify documents? Would I risk my career and reputation? Risk the possibility of jail?"

His mouth hardened in a grimly determined line. "In a heartbeat. I will not let Margo Bailey die. Now I need your help. And I would be making you an accomplice. For that, I am very sorry."

Ruby was shaking her head in disbelief.

The doctor nodded understandingly. "Maybe after the operation, you will need to report my actions to the authorities. I will understand. I will absolutely understand if you feel that is what you need to do. But I beg of you, let me save this girl's life. Let me save Margo Bailey and then do as you must."

Though bewildered, Ruby's loyalty was destined to win out. This was her first job out of college, and she was a bit dazzled by the medical genius of her boss and the extraordinary life-saving miracles he performed. She sucked in a deep breath and nodded slowly.

"I'll be ready to operate by ten p.m. There's not a moment to waste. Go get her."

CHAPTER TWO

At some point, all responsible adults have to tackle the morbid challenge of writing their last will and testament. It was a practice that Margo Bailey was an old pro at by her early adult years, having written her first will at the tender age of eight and having revised it yearly ever since.

She had inherited her mother's congenital heart disease, the same condition that caused her mother to die during childbirth at the age of twenty-seven. Margo knew from a young age that she had suffered the same genetic defect, one that would almost certainly cut her life short. There was no guarantee as to when, but in the back of her mind, it felt reasonable to assume that she would die around the same age that her mother had.

As a young child, there was something about the age of twenty-seven that had struck Margo as so comfortingly far away. It was older than sixteen. It was older than twenty! It was an abstract day of reckoning that she convinced herself was so far away, it might never arrive. Her twelfth year took away those comforting assumptions.

There are things that just slip one's mind. Who knew her weak heart could ever be one of them? And yet, Margo was racing alongside her sister, Bette, for the bus - the one that would take them up the coast to a carnival where there was a guarantee of a Ferris wheel, mouth-watering kettle corn, pre-historic turkey legs, and a loud, intoxicating arcade. But it was a long race for the bus, and they were determined to catch it, or they'd be waiting another hour for the next one.

But Margo fell behind, and the painful pounding of her heart brought the memory of its weakness back with full force. She sank to the ground, and noted with dread panic, that it showed no sign of slowing down. Not when Bette came back to retrieve her; nor as the two waited for the ambulance together.

How could it be happening so soon? She was only twelve, and she was about to die. She would never learn how to drive. Never have a job like a real adult. Never travel out of the state. Never be kissed. (that one made her cry.) Not to mention, she had just purchased some lovely bead earrings that had yet to be assigned to a formal bequest. Bette was in such hysterics that Margo had to ask for pen and paper at the hospital to make the impromptu adjustment to her will, since Bette was hardly in a state where she would remember this final directive.

As luck would have it, Margo's time had not come. She got a few unpleasant injections, underwent a battery of tests, and spent one night at the hospital before being given the okay to go home. But not before the doctor sat down and gave her a long, stern lecture on the stupidity of taking such foolish chances with her heart. Their examinations revealed problems that qualified her for a heart transplant! But her condition wasn't as urgent as about five hundred other people on the transplant list. In other words, don't hold your breath. And stop engaging in risky behaviors.

She did remember thinking at the time, if running is too risky, then what else was too dangerous for her to do. It was a question that hung over all the future days ahead, right to the present moment.

And so the last fifteen years had passed, and never wanting to stare death so abruptly in the face again, Margo became a paragon of cautious living. Excessively so, most people would say. But the reality she lived with was hard for others to comprehend. Easy for them to be cavalier with her fragile existence. Well, Margo knew better. And she was determined to shield her heart from any dangers, shocks, anxieties, demands that could send her hurtling toward an early grave.

That meant no driving. No junk food. No tall ladders. No running. No venturing into the ocean higher than her knees. No bare feet on the beach – jellyfish were too much of a risk. No roller coasters. No scary movies. In short, nothing that would send her heart racing. Fear and caution were the twin foundations of her continued existence. Her protectors. Her bodyguards.

The most unfortunate of her self-imposed restrictions was not allowing herself to become too excited during—well, what for most people would be the throes of passion. But it's not all that passionate if one is simultaneously performing relaxation techniques in order to avoid an excessively fast heartbeat. In fact, it's a cold bucket of water in that moment of passion. At least, Margo's only two boyfriends thought so.

"Are you doing breathing exercises?" she was asked incredulously.

"I just felt my heart beating a little too fast. But I think I can keep it calm. No, no. It's not a problem. I got this."

In all fairness, she couldn't blame either of them for breaking up with her. Now, at the age of twenty-six, she was relieved that she'd never formed any lasting romantic attachment. How sad it would have been for him to suffer through her recent decline.

For the past year, there was an undeniable feeling that her heart was getting weaker. The tiredness that she just couldn't shake off. A checkup with Dr. Svenson six months ago had confirmed her worst fears.

"Your heart valves are deteriorating at an accelerated pace," Dr. Svenson had informed Margo reluctantly. "Which will qualify you for the very top of the transplant list. That's the good news."

"And the bad news?"

"We're going to be needing that transplant soon. Very, very soon."

There was no need for him to elaborate on the consequences. Margo's mother had died at the age of twenty-seven. And likely, so would she.

*****

Consequently, every new purchase and acquisition had to be weighed against the probability that Margo's days were numbered and that her sister, Bette, her perennial beneficiary, would spend far more years with these items than she would. As they stood before a window display with an exquisite rose quartz pendant, Margo knew she could only think about buying it if it was something that Bette would love for herself.

"I bet it would look great on you," she told her sister.

"Don't you dare buy that unless you think that it's going to look great on you," Bette scolded. "And of course it's going to look great on you. You should absolutely get it."

Margo looked longingly back at the necklace. Then at her sister and herself reflected in the store's window. Even though they had different fathers, there was a strong family resemblance. As a die-hard movie buff, Margo was forever describing people's looks by way of their celebrity doppelgangers. Her own wavy dark hair and heart-shaped face had prompted comparisons to Maggie Gyllenhaal—admittedly, a much paler, less vibrant version, particularly these past few months. Bette was a bit more reminiscent of Marisa Tomei.

Bette was much more fashionably attired—with a bit more *savoir faire*, as she would have put it. Bette studied French wardrobe websites and had taught herself to speak a dozen different languages, maybe only twenty phrases in each, but one day, she intended to travel and wanted to be prepared.

The proprietor, Delphine Sykes, appeared at the entrance. Delphine was an auburn-haired Olympia Dukakis, circa *Moonstruck*. In her late fifties, she was wonderfully sociable and unnervingly observant.

"Are you girls gonna stand out here forever?" Delphine scolded "Come on in. I don't bite."

"Hi. Oh, we were just . . ." Margo fumbled.

With Delphine's watchful eyes upon her, Margo remembered that Delphine had a certain reputation around town. Like a multitude of women over the age of fifty in Oyster Cove, she was thought by some to be a witch. Not that Margo bought into such nonsense. And she certainly didn't want Delphine to think that she did.

"Sure. I'm Margo, by the way."

"*Margo's Movie House*," Delphine responded.

"That's me. And this is my sister Bette. It's with an E, and it's pronounced like Bette Davis. We were just about to come in to take a look."

Delphine raised an eyebrow. She wasn't so sure that they had been about to come in, but she'd take it. She loved company. The three of them retreated into her shop. It was a kaleidoscope of color with murals, paintings, sculptures, and fabric art, all an alluring backdrop for the jewelry, which still managed to shine in a mesmerizing fashion.

sometimes felt guilty that Bette didn't receive a share and indeed had tried to give her one, which Bette wouldn't hear of . . . perhaps because she felt guilty that she got the good heart.

Margo had used her inheritance after her great aunt died to buy an art house movie theater. It was located about six blocks away from the beach and luckily situated right between Clarissa Butler's wildly popular eatery, *The Clam Shack* and a large coffeehouse on the other side. The three businesses boosted one another's bottom line considerably with customers meandering from one place to the next. Clarissa and Margo had even come up with a joint promotion for slow winter weekdays—Tuesdays through Thursdays—the daily fish special at Clarissa's and your choice of movie for fifteen dollars.

As Margo walked through the scenic streets of Oyster Bay, one colorful storefront after another caught her eye. The upside about a town that had evolved around impoverished artists was that they had left their creative mark at every turn . . . painting, sculpting, mosaic art, 3D figures jutting out from the building. . .

Her own theater was no exception. As she approached it on this particular day, she admired its Art Deco exterior for the umpteenth time. A lot of those vintage pieces had taken months to track down. And the twin pastel green, pink, and black mosaics of the Chrysler building that stood at either side of the entrance were the work of a local artist whom Margo wanted to hug every time she saw her.

There was more artwork inside. Margo so admired and wanted to support the local artists that she had dedicated a large portion of the interior wall space to effectively function as an art gallery, changing monthly to showcase as much of the local talent as possible and usually attracting a small handful of commissions for every exhibit.

It was a small theater, but Margo wanted it to be a homey, sociable place. She had three separate sitting areas with inviting sofas and plump chairs in the waiting area. It was nice to see people meet for their film half an hour early, just hanging out in those cozy waiting areas.

It made for great people watching—particularly, the families. Margo knew that a husband and children were not in the cards for her. Nor traveling, adventurous activities, or the sheer joy of planning for the future. But she contented herself with every ounce of vicarious enjoyment that was to be had from watching others live out their energetic, sprawling, lucky, lucky lives.

And it wasn't as if her life hadn't come with some satisfactions. The theater itself was her proudest achievement. It consisted of three viewing rooms, one dedicated to foreign language films, one to indie films—and both of these with renovated booths and tables and a BYOB policy—and the largest room was dedicated to golden oldies. Although, customers were constantly debating whether a film that came out in 1980 could be called an 'oldie'. Well, that was before Margo was born, so it certainly felt old. *Classics* was probably a less problematic term.

It was the true oldies that had been her mother's favorites. The mother she had never known. But her great aunt had told her as much as she could remember about Nora Bailey. Nora's all-time favorite film was *All About Eve*. Hence, she named her first child after Bette Davis and planned to name her second after the great and fictitious Margo Channing, the middle-aged, sharp-tongued whirlwind whose unimaginable self-possession and confidence never failed to leave Margo feeling a tad inadequate for failing to live up to her namesake.

Margo and Bette had watched the film over and over, trying to reach out for any possible connection to their late mother. Which naturally led to all Bette Davis films, weeping buckets during *Dark Victory*, and the belief that their mother's personality was something akin to Charlotte Vale from *Now, Voyager*—after she grew a spine, of course. It was that film that convinced Bette that she needed to see Rio de Janeiro and then the whole world.

Davis was followed by Katherine Hepburn and then Cary Grant—*Holiday!*—and by then, they were hooked. When it came to choosing what kind of business for Margo to start, it was a no-brainer. She called it *Margo's Movie House*. Not self-named for the normal gratifications of ego, but to create something that would outlive her short life. Something that would say, *Margo Bailey was here*.

*****

"We've got five bucks riding on this, and if anyone knows this, it's going to be you," a flirtatious college boy told Margo.

His smug buddy waited expectantly. Margo shook her head. She was expected to know everything about movie trivia. Hadn't these fellas heard of Google?

"Okay, before Gwyneth Paltrow and *that guy* were in *Shakespeare in Love*—who was supposed to play those parts?"

Margo sighed with relief—an easy one. "Julia Roberts and Daniel Day Lewis."

The smug guy's mouth dropped open. "You gotta be kiddin'."

"Popcorn's on you, buddy," the first guy crowed. "I know my movies."

"You certainly do," Margo said, trying not to ogle this fellow's broad shoulders. He was way too young for her. And she certainly wasn't available for a romantic development.

"Excuse me! Excuse me!" Ruby Townsend practically shoved those young men out of the way. She was breathing so hard from a record-breaking sprint from her car that she could barely get her next words out.

She was a very familiar face to Margo—Doctor Svenson's young assistant. She had dropped by to catch a movie on a number of earlier occasions. But why was she in such a lather today? Ruby locked eyes with Margo, who let out a gasp as she realized the only possible reason for such a dramatic entrance.

"We have a heart for you, Margo. Surgery's at ten p.m. You need to leave. You need to leave right now."

In a daze, Margo asked Ted, the projectionist, to take over the ticket booth, and she let Ruby drag her out to the car. For the *study. But look at these unworthy girls who were receiving her organs. Her powers were being scattered, diluted amongst these weak, slow, clueless, pathetic girls.*

"You're keeping the brain?" another doctor wondered.

Dr. Svenson had been obligated to recruit surgical teams from all over Cape Cod and the Boston area to complete this marathon of operations.

"Scientific study," he answered evenly. "Her family has given consent."

"Anything special about her brain?"

"She was a remarkable woman. I think her brain is going to give us some extraordinary insights into the vast range of human potential."

All told, there were eight recipients of these lifesaving, life-changing procedures. (And eventually, there would be a ninth.) But exactly how life-changing, even Dr. Svenson could not foresee.

Lilith's interest in her body was not idle. She had been murdered. She needed to know who had done it and she needed a means of seeking sweet vengeance. But she would need earthly assistance. And who better than one of these girls who owed her their life? Oh, she would press one of them into assistance and when the time came, they would have no choice in the matter. Who would be the likeliest, strongest candidate? It was too soon to tell. First up was Margo Bailey.

*****

Even before she opened her eyes, Margo lay in the hospital bed listening to her new heart beat. Normally, this would have terrified her, primarily because so many things terrified her. But this heartbeat had a soothing and emboldening effect on her. She opened her eyes, and hands clasped together, she put her hands on top of the new organ. The area was tender, perhaps even a bit painful. Funny that she took it in stride when pain used to send her into such a panic.

More important than any discomfort was the strong, powerful rhythm beneath the skin with the dizzying promise of boundless strength and energy. Still in her dressing robe, she made her way to the door and peered into an empty hospital corridor. No one was about. The transplant operations were still ongoing and demanded everyone's attention. Margo wondered how long she'd been there. Where was the doctor? What was it like outside? All of a sudden, she just had to know.

At first, she made a slow patter across the cold floor, all the while delighting in her new heart's ability to handle all challenges. She sailed right past the front desk attendant before the woman could even react.

"Wait! Stop! Miss Bailey! Stop!"

But Margo was not inclined to turn back. These were her first moments of hope, of existing in a body that would not fail her. All the world had to be seen and felt through the eyes of this lucky new creature, this new Margo Bailey. And like a dog straining at the leash, her new heart really seemed to want to be let loose. She continued her soft jog with a loop around the hospital grounds and became aware after a few moments that there was a large group of people running and screaming behind her.

It would surely only take them a moment to catch up. Other people were always faster and stronger than herself. But the new heart urged her on and she couldn't resist. She broke into a sprint, her heart pumping as fast and as hard as she needed it to. She didn't stop until she'd arrived back at the front of the hospital, where Dr. Svenson stood, whom she made a beeline for. His mouth dropped, and Margo was thrilled to be able to share the moment with him. The doctor's eyes filled with tears and Margo threw her arms around him.

"Thank you, Dr. Svenson. Thank you for everything. I think I'm ready to go home now."

The posse that had been chasing her arrived, huffing and puffing, some collapsing on the ground. Margo noted their exhaustion with amazement. She had always a wanted a heart as strong as everyone else's. But to be stronger than others? That was a possibility she could barely comprehend. Dr. Svenson examined the healthy young woman before him. This was no ordinary success. This was the power of the witch's heart. But what lay ahead for her?

"Be careful, my dear. You don't want to overtax your new heart."

But anyone looking at her dazed and dreamy expression would suspect that Margo Bailey had no intention of slowing down. Not now.

*****

Bette was quite prepared to play the nurse for as long as need be. She had requested to take several days off work to fetch and carry meals and drinks, do the dishes, laundry, whatever she could to spare Margo from too much exertion. When she rolled out of bed the first morning after Margo's return, she tiptoed into the hallway, not wanting to wake her sister unnecessarily.

Margo's door was open and Margo was nowhere to be seen. A frantic search through the small two-story house revealed that Bette was completely alone. She ran outside frantically.

Behind their lavender gray Nantucket-style beach home, there was a sight to be seen. Margo was perched at the top of a tall ladder all the way up to the edge of the roof, and she appeared to be repairing some loose shingles.

"Margo," Bette called out softly, not wanting to startle her sister. "What on earth are you doing?"

"Good, you're up. I need to hammer this on and I was worried all the noise would wake you up."

"Are you *loco*?"

"Just give me two minutes," Margo said.

She cheerily hammered two loose shingles back into place and swiftly descended the ladder without a moment of hesitation.

"Now we won't need to have to pay to have it repaired. It was a really easy fix."

"You could have fallen," Bette fussed.

"But it's a really good ladder. And I've got good balance."

"You just had a life-saving operation. I don't know if this is really the right time to turn into a daredevil."

"I just wanted to test myself. To test the new heart. Just to stand on the bottom rung, and if that was okay, to go up one more rung, and then one more. I knew I could stop as soon as I got scared. I never thought I'd make it past four rungs. And then all of a sudden, I was touching the roof!"

"But you always said that ladders make you nervous."

"They did. They absolutely did. And my old heart couldn't stand being nervous. But Bette . . . my new heart! I think it will stay strong even if I'm doing something scary. The thing is . . . this wasn't a very good test for it because it just didn't feel all that scary."

"Oh, it's bad enough. You'd never get me up that ladder."

Margo tried to suppress a big smile, but to no avail. She could handle something her older sister could not!

Bette shook her head. "I'm starting to think I didn't really need to take any days off."

"Oh, no. I'm glad you did. After breakfast, I was hoping I could get a little practice . . . driving your car."

"My car! My . . . Margo, you haven't driven since you were sixteen."

"Yeah, but I still have that license. And it's about to expire, so I could use a little practice before I take another driving test."

"Do you remember the last time I took you driving? I kept telling you . . . a little bit faster, try to go faster. And you said, I am going faster. And I said, you really need to try to get up to twenty-five miles an hour."

"Very funny. I was sixteen and I didn't know how to do anything. Things are different now. Way different."

"All right, but only if we go out somewhere secluded. Nothing to run into. And if we run into something, you pay all the damages. I must be out of my mind."

Bette was only pretending to be put out. The sight of her fragile little sister tackling the daily chores of life with gusto was a thrilling contrast to the walking on eggshells existence of their past twenty years together.

So much for seclusion. Not a chance. Margo wanted to zip up and down the freeway. "Let's have lunch in Falmouth and then drive back."

"Margo, you're not just stronger, you're . . . different."

"I'm not different. I just don't need to be so careful anymore. I don't need to keep worrying about the things I can't do."

"So . . . the Prada glasses?"

The green tinted, black and silver rimmed designer sunglasses were Margo's prized possession, certainly her most expensive indulgence.

Like all other acquisitions, it was bought on the understanding that Bette would inherit it after Margo's untimely death. They were super cool. And Margo had always known they would look fantastic on her sister.

"Forget about it. *My* glasses! *My* glasses! I'm going to be needing them for the foreseeable future. And for the unforeseeable future. As a matter of fact, I intend to wear those glasses to my seventieth birthday party. So, you just get your beady eyes off them."

The sisters laughed and couldn't stop. What a turning point for Margo. Such confidence about the future, and why not? Her endurance was remarkable and her frame of mind followed suit. There would be no more grim updates to her will. There was no reason to think that her strength and vitality were going to wane anytime in the near future.

Lilith was not so impressed. Strength. Endurance. Energy. Those were small matters. Though she smugly remembered hearing all the world around her complaining of being tired and knowing that to be a completely foreign sensation to her—as was fear, which she was happy to see the girl slowly discovering. But endurance and attitude were not going to be enough, not even close. This girl needed skills. And with Margo not being connected to the witch community, their development was going to require some planning.

*****

It was a big day for Lilith Hazelwood. In the morning, there was to be an estate sale of her lifelong home and all its possessions. In the afternoon was to be her funeral. It was actually quite an unofficial estate sale. But it was a long-standing tradition for witches in this community to protect their practices and secrets by stripping the home of their dead of any incriminating evidence of magic crystals, wands, herbs, and most especially spell books, all the tools of the trade, so to speak. Not that the average citizen of Oyster Cove would be able to accomplish much with them, but such findings often led to public hysteria. Besides which, there might be some unexpected treasures that they could actually use.

There were some dozen witches milling around the large house. None of them had been inside before. It was unexpectedly cheerful. They would've bet good money that Lilith's home would reek of gloom. Instead, it was tidy, cozy, even downright tastefully decorated. The English country design appeared to belie a nostalgia for times gone by . . . plush velvet sofas, gleaming polished wood, a large brick fireplace, and, most surprising, floor to ceiling bookcases, filled with vintage reading. Could Lilith possibly have admired the words of lowly humans? Or was the impressive collection just for ambiance?

None of the witches there had actually been friends of Lilith. She had made it very clear throughout her long life that she had no need of their friendship. Some disliked her, but most admired her from a fearful distance as the pinnacle of witchly accomplishment.

There were a couple of dozen spell books, which were quickly spirited away, but not much else, and that was a testament to Lilith's innate powers. She had not required the enhancements that most of them used to channel their strengths such as talismans or amulets. Her abilities emanated from her mind and body with little need for assistance.

By the time the witches allowed the general public to come in, they had satisfied themselves that all signs of their community were safely under wraps. Most of them had made their exit by mid-morning. After all, they had a funeral to attend. Being such a small community, it was obligatory to pay one's respects—even though no one could have been entirely sure that Lilith would have attended theirs.

But a few lingered behind and were still there when Margo and Dr. Svenson entered. Margo had begged the doctor for some kind of information or connection to the woman whose death had given her this powerful new lease on life.

She entered the house awestruck, overcome with reverence and gratitude. All the while that she'd been waiting for a heart to be available, she had never lost sight of the fact that someone would have to lose their life in order for her to have a chance to live. Now she was standing in the home of the woman who had made that sacrifice. There would never be an opportunity to meet her or to thank her, nor even to thank her relatives, since the doctor said there were none. But she did want to find a keepsake, something to remind her of the woman to whom she was indebted.

She wandered out onto the back porch and spotted the perfect thing, a blue vase that reminded her of a seashell. She would give it a place of honor in her own home. As she was about to reenter the house, she was met at the back door by Delphine Sykes, who was looking at her with the oddest expression.

"My dear girl, you're looking so well. You're practically glowing. This is quite some difference from when I saw you last."

Margo nodded happily. "That seems a lifetime ago."

Delphine drew closer, and her mouth dropped in amazement. "I had no idea that you're one of us. How on earth did I miss it?"

Margo tilted her head in confusion. "One of us? Who is *us*?"

Delphine examined her sharply. "Your powers. I can always sense them, but . . ." It was clear that Margo had no idea what she was talking about. "What has happened to you, Margo?"

"I got a heart transplant. I'm going to be healthy now, as healthy as anyone else. Maybe even healthier. I came here today . . . I don't know, I guess it may sound silly, but it was the woman who lived here whose heart I have. Her name was Lilith Hazelwood. Did you know her?"

Delphine shook her head in amazement. "Indeed I did, my dear. We were acquaintances of long standing."

"I'm very sorry for your loss. I'd love to hear more about her one day, when you're ready."

"I had no idea that Lilith Hazelwood was an organ donor," Delphine said pointedly. "Who conducted the operation?"

"Dr. Svenson," Margo said proudly. "He's right in the next room."

"I must congratulate him on his stunning success," Delphine said innocently. "He must be a very talented man."

"Yeah, you should do that. I keep thanking him over and over, but he's just amazing. He should hear it from someone else too."

Delphine left to accost the good doctor, who was in Lilith's kitchen, hoping to find some clues to her unusual existence. After all, it was he who had made her body a part of so many lives. He didn't regret it for a moment, but he did wonder about the ramifications. Hmm. Graham crackers and Nutella in her cupboard, much like his own pantry. Somehow, he never would have figured Lilith for a sweet tooth.

"Dr. Svenson. Allow me to introduce myself. My name is Delphine Sykes. And I would like to know who gave you permission to slice and dice and dismember Lilith Hazelwood? Is it your policy to disregard conventional protocol when it comes to members of a particular community?"

Dr. Svenson's eyes flew wide open. "I take it that you are a member of this community."

"I am."

"Was Lilith a friend of yours?"

"Lilith Hazelwood did not have friends. She had no need of friends."

"And Margo Bailey? You know her well?"

"Not well at all. I only knew that she was doing very poorly, and now . . ."

"Yes, now. You see how she is now. How beautifully she is doing now. I have no apologies for my actions, and I'm prepared to accept any and all consequences from the authorities, as well as from yourself. The health and future of that girl are the only justifications I needed."

"Bit of an outlaw, aren't we, Dr. Svenson?" Delphine mused.

"She has a good heart now, and I suspect you also have a good heart."

The doctor's affection for Margo was enough to dissolve Delphine's irritation.

Delphine sighed. "If you'll excuse me, Doctor, I have a funeral to attend."

CHAPTER FOUR

The funeral was surprisingly well-attended by some thirty witches, which was almost the entire witch population of Oyster Cove. Lilith herself hovered nearby, which was to be expected. A handful of attendees were keenly aware her presence. It was not such an unusual thing to be able to see ghosts. Much rarer was the ability to hear them. Many who did not have this ability counted themselves lucky. Who wanted to spend their time talking to unhappy ghosts? And if a ghost is hanging around, they're probably unhappy.

Delphine was not so lucky. Lilith made a beeline for her.

"Delphine Sykes. I call on your assistance."

"Lilith. I can't tell you how . . . how shocked we all were to find out . . . umm . . . assistance?"

"You have met this girl, Margo Bailey. My body lives on. My heart still beats. My powers are still there. Under the surface, but weak, dormant, untrained. You must teach her spells, tools, mind, emotion, and control. She will never have my full abilities, of course. But to even have a fraction of

them is a seed that might grow to unimaginable size, given the right guidance."

"But why do you care? Who is this girl to you? Unless I'm mistaken, she is a complete stranger. How can you benefit from this? And why are you still here?"

"Have you not wondered about my demise? I hope you're not foolish enough to think that it was a natural accident. Dark forces were at work . . . an enemy I wasn't even aware of. But I must know. I must find out who, and I must have my vengeance. I call on this favor from someone who owes me her life."

"I?"

"The girl."

"Oh, I don't know, Lilith. She seems an unlikely candidate. There's very little darkness in her. And I think she has certainly experienced enough trauma in her young life already."

"What of your own life?" Lilith demanded. "There's something out there powerful enough to have killed me. Surely, you can take an interest in that."

Delphine couldn't deny it. "Yes, that is something that poses a danger to all of us. Anyone who was able to kill you may strike any of us, at any time. Of course we need to know. But Margo Bailey doesn't deserve to be in danger. And it will take some time, at any rate, for her to learn and accept what she is now. She is likely to be frightened. There's no guarantee that she can handle it."

"She will. You will see to that. Do not let me down, Delphine Sykes."

At that moment, both of their attention was drawn to a new arrival to the funeral. It was Fiona Skretting, long regarded as the second-most powerful witch in Oyster Cove. Only now, she was indisputably the first. She *stood at a distance from the other attendees and looked upon the proceedings with what could only be regarded as smug satisfaction. Delphine and Lilith regarded one another. Lilith bristled.*

"I will try," Delphine promised.

*****

Margo had returned to work almost immediately. Convalescence was unnecessary, and she was infused with health and energy, so why not? At the end of this particular evening, it occurred to her that she had the strength to take care of many of the things that she'd delegated before, for fear of exertion. Such as the garbage.

It had been a long time since she was in the back alley. As she was about to fling the garbage bags into the small dumpster, she heard a small screech near her foot. A beige and white tabby cat darted away.

"Oh. Sorry about that."

She noticed the smell wafting from a bag of trash from *The Clam Shack*, smells that must have been irresistible to a feline.

"All right, all right, I'll give you a hand."

Hmmm. Margo had never given cats much thought. Dogs, on the other hand . . . she had wanted a dog since she was very young. But her great aunt wouldn't hear of it. It was bad enough that she was raising two young girls at her advanced age. She certainly wasn't going to add a dog to the mix.

Their neighbor had gotten himself a sweet little dog. Margo hadn't even known what type of dog it was. Some mix that even

Mr. Phillips wasn't sure about, since it had been a rescue dog. A little terrier in it, for sure. It was a nice, manageable size—perfect for an eighty-two-year-old man who could pick him up, if necessary, and also not have to contend with a strong behemoth dragging him around the neighborhood.

But Margo admired them from a distance. After she was grown, she was so certain for a while that she would get one, but she got sidetracked by opening up the theater. And then, two years ago, Mr. Phillips died. Oh, how forlorn that dog had been. One of the neighbors volunteered to take him in for a while, but he was constantly jumping their fence or breaking away from its leash to stand on his old front porch and howl at the front door.

What heartache for the poor thing. First to endure his first bout of abandonment before his rescue. Then to lose the security and love he had found with Mr. Phillips. Margo so wanted to take him in and provide him with a warm, secure place to the end of his days. Except . . . she had had no assurance that he wouldn't outlive her. How awful that would be for a poor dog who had already been through so much. To deal with the death and disappearance of yet another owner! She couldn't do it to him.

So she watched with mixed feelings as an ad at the local café landed him a permanent home across town. Good for him. At the time, she also thought—good for her, too. Another important lesson learned. No long-term commitments. No deep attachments. No setting anyone up to be devastated by her departure. Not if it could be helped.

But now, all the old concerns and restrictions were falling away. She could get a dog if she wanted to. Too bad she wasn't really interested in a cat. She carefully opened the garbage bag and pulled out a nice piece of fish.

"Here you go, buddy. You'll like this."

The cat paced before her nervously, sometimes advancing and snarling and then backing away, looking at her helplessly.

"What is your problem? This even looks good to me, and it's garbage."

Sighing, she got on her knees and held out the piece of fish. To her surprise, the cat came to her immediately and wolfed it out of her hands.

"That's what I thought. Shall I see if we can find another one?" She stood up and the cat screeched again and ran away.

"This is why I never wanted a cat," Margo said. "You're crazy."

She located another piece of fish, but again, the cat paced back and forth, moving forward and screeching at her and backing away. Weird. Again, she got on her knees, and the cat ran in to gulp down his second course. Margo stood again, to be met with more screeching.

It only took a few more repeats of the odd pattern of behavior for Margo to figure out the rhyme and reason behind it. Any time her foot came near him, the cat was terrified. When she reached for him with her hand for food, he was okay, and when she reached for him with her hand to pet him, he was okay, but coming too close to her foot put him on high alert.

This cat had been kicked. So often, that human feet terrified him. How awful. He needed someone to be kind to him. And in that moment, Margo became a cat person. She found another small handful of food, gathered the cat tightly in her arms, and took a cab home.

*****

The newcomer gingerly explored his new surroundings. Their living room was a pillow and cushion filled shabby chic decor, which had no shortage of soft things for a feline to nestle on. Thankfully, there was no black furniture, or they'd have had to start vacuuming twice a day. Instead, the cat complemented the green and beige color scheme rather nicely.

Bette shook her head. "It's a cat. It was supposed to be a dog. It was always all about the dog."

"I know. But he shouldn't be out on his own without anyone to take care of him. He's so scared of everything."

"That's a good name for him—Scaredy-Cat."

"Lovely. No, you are not going to call him Scaredy-Cat. He's been through enough. I can't think of a decent name though. You have to help me out."

Bette looked off into the distance. She had quite a good imagination. Margo was sure she would nail it.

"Got it! New heart. New cat. Newhart. It's a name! Perfect to celebrate all your new beginnings."

"You mean Newheart. Is that with two *E*s?"

"No, you don't want him to be a freak. Just regular old Newhart."

It was fitting, Margo couldn't deny. New cat. New life. Newhart.

*****

Margo had just left the veterinarian. He'd given Newhart a full checkup and a psychological screening. Being the victim of abuse and abandonment, Newhart was filled with insecurity. Margo would need to keep him close and provide constant reassurance. Even leaving him alone at home was probably not a good idea at this stage of his development. They really needed to bond.

So, it was with Newhart tucked in his cozy little carrier that Margo strolled down the boardwalk. A figure that she spotted several yards ahead made her come to a dead stop. It was Russell Knox, a face from her past that never failed to fill her with shame. She'd only seen him at a distance in the last few years, and before then, not since high school.

The day seared into her memory was of Russell being bullied by three larger kids as she was headed home from the library. They were from her eighth-grade cohort, with Russell being a year younger than the rest. Such moments were the worst thing about her old weak heart. It wouldn't have been so bad if she were the only one to suffer from her limitations. But in that moment, she hadn't had the strength or the courage to offer help when it was badly needed.

They were poking fun at his clothes, of all things. It appeared his crime was having pants that were too short and a little too tight. Margo had suspected that this particular fashion crime owed more to pinched financial resources than to lack of fashion acumen. But those oafs hadn't cared. They seemed delighted to stumble across something worthy of their scorn.

When Margo saw the pushing and shoving begin, she had felt her heart begin yet another alarming escalation. It had only been about one year since her doctor had made his frightening prognosis and laid down the law about taking it easy. The thought of stepping closer to intervene only resulted in deathly fight or flight palpitations.

Why did Russell have to catch her eye as she scurried past? His eyes were filled with fear and anger. Anger at Margo, as well as at his tormentors, for not having the courage to stop and help. She had played that day over and over in her mind so many times. What a useless creature her heart had made her.

After high school, Russell disappeared. College, no doubt. He had come back two years ago with a girlfriend. He opened up a tapas restaurant, *Barcelona*, the only one of its kind in town. Apparently, it was a roaring success. Margo was glad for him. Everything seemed to be working out great for him despite a bullied youth.

She still carried such regrets from that day. And she so wanted to speak to him. Did he resent her? Had he forgiven her? She had never really forgiven herself. If she could just talk to him . . . perhaps she could get some kind of closure, if nothing else.

As she approached, she could see that Russell had turned into a fine, handsome young man—she was going to go with . . . Ewan McGregor. As she came within ten yards of him, she was startled by a black-and-white police car rushing to his side. Two police officers leapt out, flashed their badges, and proceeded to handcuff him.

As Margo cautiously crept closer, she could hear Russell being read his rights.

"Do you understand these rights as I've read them to you?"

Russell nodded in a daze. Again, he locked eyes with Margo. His face was filled with panic and confusion. They pushed him down into their car and zoomed away. The feeling of helplessness that descended on Margo was so unbearable, she shoved it away with as much force as she could. Russell Knox was in terrible, terrible trouble. This time, she had to do something about it.

*****

A man had been murdered in Russell Knox's restaurant. Poisoned, actually. Margo heard all the details from her business neighbor, Clarissa of *The Clam Shack*.

"I know this guy's brother. Walter, he's my accountant. Geez, this is unbelievable. I've actually eaten at that restaurant. Though I suppose nothing would have happened to me."

"You mean, you've never gotten food poisoning?" Margo wondered.

"It wasn't food poisoning. It was poisoning, poisoning put deliberately into the dead guy's food. This isn't negligence. He's up for first-degree murder."

That was insane. Although Margo didn't know Russell well, she still had such a feel for his general decency, even from a distance. It just didn't ring true with everything else that she'd heard about him. How could he be a cold-blooded murderer?

It's true that he hadn't had a very good childhood. He was poor. He was bullied. Had he been bullied so many years that he was filled with repressed rage? And oh, dear, could Margo have changed the course of his life by showing more courage on that critical day, so long ago?

*****

Two days later, Margo couldn't sit still any longer. Even though they had no real connection and had never had a friendship, she had to speak to Russell. She went to the police station, which also contained the local jail, and was relieved that they could accommodate her with a visit on the spot. Looking around the station, she spotted a decidedly new face. At a glance, she would say a young Mark Ruffalo. Where'd he come from?

Margo was seated in a low security visitors' room, and she waited nervously for Russell to enter. The look on his face was of pleasant bewilderment.

"Wow! This is a surprise. I mean super, super surprised. Margo Bailey. Hey, you know something? I just heard last week about your new heart. That's terrific. It really is. I'm so glad for you. I really am."

Margo's eyes filled with tears. This was not the first thing she expected to hear from Russell. He was in such horrible trouble and had all the reason in the world to resent her, hold a grudge. But her good news had momentarily transported him away from his own troubled situation.

"Russell, please tell me what happened. Maybe I can help."

"Four days ago, a man died in my restaurant. It just looked like a tragic allergic reaction, you know—vomiting, seizure, coma. He died soon after he got to the hospital. Of course, everyone suspected food poisoning, but that's really not how food poisoning works. Anyway, they found traces of arsenic on my coat. And here's the insane thing . . . a bottle of arsenic in my car. Someone put a freakin' bottle of arsenic in my car to make it look like I did this."

"Who? Who would have done such a thing? Margo marveled.

"You don't believe that—"

"No, of course not. It just sounds—"

"I know how it sounds."

"The man who was killed . . . who was he? Did you know him?"

"His name was Julian Meeks, just a summer resident. I had never seen the guy before in my life. First time at the restaurant. His whole family was there. What a horrible thing for them to see, right?"

'Mark Ruffalo' was at the door. "You have another visitor."

Margo pushed her chair back. "I should leave."

"Stay. Please."

In came Walter Knox, brother and accountant, with a computer tucked under his arm.

"Oh, I'm not your guest. Grandpa is your guest. I'm going to Skype him in. You just helped push him a few feet closer to his grave, which I'm sure suits you just fine." Walter turned to Margo. "Junior, here, is the sole beneficiary of my grandpa's estate. How d'ya like that? Nothing for me. Everything going to him."

"That was Grandpa's decision. He knew you'd gamble it all away, Walter. That's on you. And you know he's right."

Walter proceeded to set up the Skype. "So the prodigal grandson has been doing everything he can to get our grandpa off life support equipment so that he can get his hands on that money."

"That is such garbage! Grandpa is either in a doped up stupor with his meds or he's in horrible pain."

"Here we go. Time for a little karma. Hey, Grandpa. I have Russell here for you." He turned the computer in Russell's direction. Margo heard the weak, angry voice of an elderly man.

"You've brought the worst shame to our family, Russell. I never want to lay eyes on you again. I've had my lawyer take you out of the will. Everything's going to Walter. You hear that? You're not going to be rewarded for murder. I just wish I hadn't lived long enough to see this day. I need my pills. Where are my pills? I need to sleep. I can't think about this anymore."

"I didn't do it! I didn't do it! Grandpa, you've gotta believe me."

Walter snapped the computer shut. "I don't need to see you again either. If you're waiting for bail, don't hold your breath."

Russell and Margo exchanged an agonized look.

'Mark Ruffalo' appeared at the door. "Ma'am, it's time to leave."

As Margo rose to her feet, it dawned on her that for over a week now, she'd been floating on air with the joy and promise of new life and new hope. And here was someone whose life was crashing to an end. It was unbearably unfair. With old, ugly feelings of helplessness descending on her, she stumbled away.

CHAPTER FIVE

B ack at home, Bette was trying to win Newhart's favor with some crunchy kitty snacks, which he devoured happily—then he would always wind up back in Margo's lap.

"What am I, chopped liver?" Bette groused.

"If you were chopped liver, you would definitely be his favorite," Margo noted.

"Hmmph! So, Russell Knox. Bottle of poison in his car? Sounds guilty."

"But why? What could possibly be the motive? It's just bad for business, especially for a food business, for a man to get poisoned by his food. It's dumb. It's not a smart way to commit murder. It's guaranteed to lose business."

"It's a shame. That tapas place. Yummy tapas. Now I guess we'll never go."

"He says he was framed. I guess everyone says that. But Bette, what if he was?"

"Like you said, he's a bullied guy who finally snapped."

"I'm no detective, but seriously, where is the motive? A man was deliberately killed by someone who hated him."

"Nothing you can do. The police are on it, so stop obsessing. It's been so nice to see you in a good mood and feeling so healthy. Let's just be happy about that."

"You're right. Absolutely right. My life is finally great."

Newhart flipped over in her lap and waited for his tummy rub. Margo scoffed, but obliged.

"This is your third tummy rub today. I hope you know this is *it*."

Newhart was no longer scared or hungry. At least Margo had been able to rescue a cat. Russell Knox was beyond her help. A hopeless case.

*****

Margo had gotten in the habit of taking Newhart to work. After the last shows began, she would let him run around the lobby. Not much choice, really. He couldn't be left at home alone. She tried it once, and boy, did he go crazy. He threw pillows all over the place and got into the hall closet and started ripping things up. The vet had warned her about this behavior. Apparently, animals generally hate being left alone.

For the past few years, Margo had taken a cab home, partially to save herself from overexertion but also because nighttime is when all the scary, bad things happened, wasn't it? In Oyster Cove, the crime rate ran to extremes. It was murder or nothing.

Still, the long walk home had felt so ominous that she could never attempt it.

But tonight, the darkness, the moon, and the cool breeze were irresistible.

"You sure?" The cab driver asked. "Someone gonna pick you up?"

"I'm walking. I'm fine."

"That's an awful long walk."

Margo was getting impatient. "I'm never going to need a cab again. Never. Ever. Not even in the pouring rain." She nodded emphatically.

The driver shrugged. Oh, well. The steady fare had been good while it lasted. But it sure was nice to see her so energetic.

Lilith nodded approvingly. "Rightfully so. There's nothing like the night." Her own powers had always been at their peak in the dead of night. It was likely the same would be true for Margo. But where was that Delphine? Shirking her orders. Lilith was getting very impatient for Margo's education to begin.

The beach looked so lovely and different at night. Margo stopped to see the moonlight sparkle across the waves. Filled with euphoria, she was so happy that she could . . . she could do a cartwheel. Not that she had ever been able to do a cartwheel, but that was her old life. Today, she refused to be daunted by simple ordinary things.

And so she gave it a try. How hard could it be? She landed on her butt. Ouch! She laughed at what a ridiculous sight she must have made. Yes, she could feel the pain. But pain didn't scare her anymore. She was willing to go for another try. Followed by another rough landing. Thank goodness for the sand.

"Excuse me, ma'am. Can I help you?"

Margo swirled around, startled. It was 'Mark Ruffalo' from the police station. She looked at him skeptically.

"I don't know. Can you do a cartwheel?"

"Umm. I can't say that is in my area of expertise."

"Then no, you can't help me."

"I can do . . . other things. I can wrestle a man twice my size to the ground. I can hit the carotid artery with just the right amount of force to disable someone without killing them."

"Impressive. Have you thought about hiring yourself out for children's parties?"

"Well, it's just all part of my practical training."

"Listen, Mr. Lethal Weapon. Clearly, we are not on the same page. I was in a cartwheel kind of mood and having a lovely evening."

"It was just so dark . . . and late. Probably not a good idea for young ladies to be walking around late at night."

Margo bristled. She had been trying so hard to shake off all of those old fears and paranoias. The last thing she needed was someone telling her that she couldn't walk home alone at night. Margo never allowed herself to get this annoyed. She'd always been worried that getting mad would stress her old heart. Now, she had to admit, it felt good to let it fly without censoring herself.

"I know the police like to send someone to patrol the beach at night. But that's to make the tourists feel better. I've lived in this town my whole life. It's perfectly safe. Except the occasional murder. Which never happens on the beach. You're new here, aren't you?"

"Yes, ma'am. Finn Cochran is the name. Yeah, I just took an early retirement from federal service after failing to dodge one too many bullets. Thought I'd try something a little quiet and uneventful, which Oyster Cove is, except for the poisoning murder." He cleared his throat. "I take it that Russell Knox is a friend of yours? I was there when you stopped by for a visit."

"Not a good friend. Just old acquaintances. Sort of. Not really. I don't think we ever even spoke to one to one another before that day at the jail. By the way, how's that whole case going?"

"Date for trial should be set by the end of the week."

"No, I mean, how are things progressing with locating other suspects?"

"Well, there aren't any."

"What if someone else did it?"

"It seems we have pretty conclusive evidence."

"He says someone is framing him."

"That's what everyone says."

Margo glared at him and grabbed Newhart's cage.

"I know it must be hard to think about a friend doing something like that," Finn conceded.

"He's not my friend. Which I just told you. If you can't pay attention to something like that, how can you possibly be conducting a careful investigation? Russell's life is at stake. He hasn't been proven guilty, and you're not even looking for other suspects."

"Perhaps we could discuss this matter over a latte."

Margo scoffed and stormed away, clutching Newhart's case. Finn flinched. No wonder he was still single.

*****

The big question Margo had was, did Julian Meeks have any enemies? Only his family would know for sure. Apparently, they owned a huge six-bedroom house, and the multi-generational clan spent much of every summer there, with a few excursions back to Boston for business.

Margo needed to talk to them. But not as Russell's friend. That, she would have to keep under wraps. She pulled her normally loose hair into a tight bun and pulled out a navy linen suit normally relegated for small business conferences and meetings with her banker. This was going to be sad, no doubt. The family would still be shocked and grieving. But this was for their benefit as well. They would want the rightful person to be behind bars.

The man who opened the door bore a strong resemblance to John Goodman.

"Yeah?" he said gruffly.

"Hi. I'm Margo Bailey. I'm so sorry to disturb you at such a difficult time. I was hoping you could provide a little information about Julian Meeks. It's so important that his rightful killer be punished."

"You from the police?"

"No, no. I'm not. I'm just trying to get the facts straight."

"Reporter, huh? What paper you with?"

As it so happened, Margo did actually have an online rag called *Margo's Movie House Gazette*. It alerted people about coming attractions, film reviews, and discounts and provided a little movie trivia.

"The *Gazette*. Could I just have a few moments of your time?"

He let Margo into the spacious house. It was a decidedly old-fashioned place, with orange, brown, and yellow flowery wallpaper, macramé wall hangings, and crocheted granny square throws—very 1970s. No doubt, its designer was matriarch Trudy Quinn, sixty-two, who sat in the living room and was either bursting into frequent sobs or dabbing her eyes dry.

"My nephew! My nephew!"

The rest of the family included Julian's brother, Carson Meeks, their cousin, Lester Quinn, who had answered the door, and his wife, Rowena Quinn, nine months pregnant. All four had been present the horrible night in question, when they saw their loved one get poisoned.

"Hey, listen up. This lady is doing a story on Jules. Just tell her what she needs to know."

"I really do apologize to all of you," Margo said sincerely. "A lot of people in Oyster Cove didn't have the chance to know Julian Meeks and it would be wonderful to see his life through his family's eyes."

"So what do you want to know?" Carson asked warily. "Favorite color? Red. Favorite team? Patriots. Height—six foot two. Blood type—B positive. Sisters—two. Brothers—one. And I'm down from one brother to none." He stopped, distraught.

"My sister's boy," Trudy agonized. "Such a sweet, sweet guy."

"Why don't we start with the basics? What was his profession?"

"We've got a big family business, the Quinns and the Meeks—we got a lot going on," Lester Quinn bragged. "We got a company that imports lumber over the border and we get it ready for builders."

"Ah, Julian worked in lumber?"

"No, I handle most of that," Lester said.

"Jules was the money guy," his brother Carson said proudly. "He was wicked smart with money."

"That's right," Lester chimed in. "He was going to be godfather to our baby because we knew if anything happened, he'd be a good provider. He knew about interest rates and all that kind of stuff."

"He was an investor?" Margo asked.

"No, well, I don't think so. He loaned money," Carson explained. "That's the biggest thing we do. Not just in Boston, but all up and down the Cape. We are the family everyone turns to. And if someone's not having any luck with the banks, they turn to us. We'll work out a good deal. Julian was the one who wrote up contracts. Had a good head for that. Lester and I were more responsible for collecting the money and straightening out the troublemakers."

Holy crap. They were loan sharks. Family business? Organized family business, perhaps? All of a sudden, John Goodman was starting to look a bit more like James Gandalfini. Not that Margo had ever seen a full episode of *The Sopranos*. It was too scary.

"These troublemaker people who didn't stick to your agreements. Is it possible that one of them might have somehow been involved in the . . . poisoning?"

"Don't see how that would be possible," Carson scoffed. "It was that restaurant owner. They caught him red-handed."

"Oh, no doubt. But . . . maybe he was in cahoots. Maybe he was used by someone else. Did Julian have any enemies?"

"He was a saint," Trudy insisted. "Lester, you and Rowena ought to name the baby after him. You really should."

Lester shook his head. "I don't think that is a good idea, ma. You'd cry every time you heard his name. It would make us all sad."

He may have had a point. Trudy burst into tears.

"I should probably go," Margo said, rising to her feet.

"That's it? Don't you have more questions?" Carson wondered.

"I already know the most important things. He was a well-loved man who was devoted to his family."

Everyone nodded, momentarily silent in their agreement.

Margo couldn't keep up the ruse any longer. She didn't want to learn what Julian Meeks's favorite colors or books were, or the fraternities he belonged to, or how much he loved football. She had far more important questions and a far more urgent interrogation to conduct.

*****

Russell was happy to see Margo again. Always good to see a friendly face, except . . . right at that moment, she wasn't looking quite as friendly as he had anticipated.

"So, Russell, you were able to start a terrific restaurant. That doesn't sound easy. I could never have started my business without my great-aunt leaving me her estate. I can't help but wonder, forgive me for saying so, but your family didn't have a lot of money. Which just makes starting your own restaurant even more of a tremendous accomplishment. I don't mean to pry, but how on earth did you raise the money to do it?"

"I borrowed it."

"From whom?"

"What?"

"From whom did you borrow it?" Margo cocked her head and stared Russell down, daring him to lie.

"Okay, okay. I knew the dead guy. I borrowed thirty thousand dollars from him. And I had twelve months to pay it back, with interest. Fifty thousand was the amount that I had to pay back."

"Russell!"

"It was doable. I mean, I had to make it work. It was the only way. Only, there was this huge snafu with my liquor license. They said I filled the application out wrong and they'd sent me a notice about that. But I never got it. And eventually, I had to re-apply. That cost me three months. My second application—same thing! How does that happen? I was frantic. I worked it out eventually, but I opened the restaurant six months later than expected. And it wasn't enough time to get fifty grand together."

"What did they say? The loan sharks?"

"I went to Julian Meeks myself to ask for more time. He asked me if I had fire insurance. I said, of course. And he said, 'if we don't get our fifty grand on the agreed upon date, your place will burn to the ground. You'll collect the insurance, and you're gonna hand over that check to me. In its entirety. Then, no broken bones. No trip to the hospital. Not everyone's cut out to be a businessman.' That's what he told me."

"Russell, you *knew* him. You lied."

"'Course I lied. Everyone is just going to see this as . . .'"

"Motive? Ya think?"

Russell flinched. "My lawyer told me not to tell anyone. He said no one would be able to see past it. Was he right?"

Margo shook her head in unhappy confusion. Why was it so difficult to accept what was so glaringly obvious right before her? No doubt, it was because of the years of guilt she had carried from that day so long ago when she was unable to help him. The case against Russell hadn't made much sense to her, previously, because it was lacking motive. She had to get away from those sad, pleading Ewan McGregor eyes before they turned her into a sap.

"I've gotta go."

Russell slumped back in his seat, defeated.

*****

Russell's secret was unlikely to remain one for long. The fact that he lied to the police about his connection to the victim—after than became known, neither the police nor jury would have any doubts about his guilt. Nor should she. Margo was well and truly bummed out. She hadn't had a clear idea about how she could help Russell, but she had wanted so badly to believe in his innocence.

She wandered distractedly down a cheerful retail street past shops like She Sells Sea Shells and Pirate Mania, with its life-sized devilishly handsome pirate mannequin greeting guests at the entrance with a drawn sword—not exactly historically correct, but the tourists didn't care. A glance across the street rewarded her with the sight of Walter Knox and a woman Margo assumed to be his wife heading into a fish and chips pub.

Walter, who had impressed her as a horribly vindictive guy, was willing to let his brother rot in jail. Margo had completely pegged him as the villain. But now, she didn't know what to think. What if she got it all wrong? At this point, she had to entertain the possibility that Russell was lying to her. Was it possible that Walter Knox might be able to supply the truth?

By the time she entered, Walter and his wife were already seated, munching on chips and chugging down tall beers. Walter was also on his cellphone. Margo quietly slipped into the adjoining booth. She wouldn't interrupt their meal but would wait till they were ready to leave. Which meant she should order something.

"Lunch special?" The waitress asked.

That would be fish and chips—fried food, which had always been a no-no. The old heart demanded a pristine diet. But Lilith Hazelwood's heart could certainly handle a little fish fry from time to time. Besides, she was hungry, and the smell from the kitchen was mouthwatering.

"Sure, and a mango sparkler."

Most people tend to raise their voices on a cellphone. Walter was no exception.

"Well, we can't pull the plug till next Wednesday. Have to wait for ten days after signing the papers. Then the doctor says he can't possibly last more than forty-eight hours after that. Which puts us at Friday. No, no. I got medical power of attorney. So all that's going to go off without a hitch. I just want to make sure there's no delay in the reading of the will, and how soon I can get a check from his estate. Could take a few weeks to sell his house. That's the big payoff for sure. But how soon can we get cash up front? Okay, I leave that in your hands. Don't let me down. Talk to you next week."

He hung up and clinked beer mugs with his wife.

"So, we good?" she asked eagerly.

"Just a few things to iron out. Harry's a good lawyer. He's on top of it. You know, the sooner the better. The important thing is that Grandpa kicks the bucket, and then you and I are on easy street."

His wife nodded. "Yeah, but what if your brother is innocent?"

"Say that happens. He goes to court and he's found innocent. Good for him. But Grandpa's six feet under, his estate is mine, and Russell is out of luck. That works for me."

Behind them, Margo had been becoming increasingly livid. So this was the devoted grandson who had scolded Russell for wanting to stop the life-support and was so indifferent to whether his brother was guilty. Just as long as the matter was decided after the grandpa was no longer around to change his will. What sort of family loyalty was that? If there were one person in the world Russell should have been able to rely on, it was this greedy, selfish, insensitive, loutish, disloyal, poor excuse for a brother.

This final grim thought was accompanied by the unexpected shattering of Margo's dinner plate and glass. Heavy ceramic and glass, filled with food and drink, just exploded on the table, untouched by anything or anyone! Margo's mouth dropped. What just happened? She looked around sharply. Earthquake? There had never been an earthquake in their neck of the woods, but if other people's plates were shattering, then perhaps there was some rational explanation.

The waitress hurried over and looked as confused as Margo felt. "What on earth happened?" She looked accusingly at Margo, who was obviously suspected of having a tantrum and destroying property.

Margo pulled $25 out of her purse, and mumbling apologies, got out as quickly as possible. Good explanation. Reasonable explanation. Rational explanation. Because the irrational and intuitive explanation was completely berserk. Her anger at Walter Knox . . . had become the shattered glass. Which made so little sense, she would never be able to mention it to anyone, not even Bette.

And then out of nowhere, a memory of something someone said recently that she hadn't been able to make head nor tails of at the time. "My dear, I had no idea you were one of us."

Margo awoke after a near-sleepless night. "My dear, I had no idea you were one of us . . . one of us . . . one of us. Her new heart beat wildly. She was about to be faced with the mother of all red pill, blue pill choices, a scene she was only familiar with secondhand, as she had previously deemed *The Matrix* as one of those films that was too heart-pounding for her.

CHAPTER SIX

Delphine was not surprised to see Margo at the entrance to her boutique. "So, you are here at last."

Margo got a sick feeling in the pit of her stomach. "What you mean?"

She knew that this was the last chance to hear something that would turn her world right side up again.

"You've come to find out who you are. What you are. Am I right?"

Margo nodded wordlessly.

"I think I'll close up shop for a little while. Why don't we take a little walk along the beach?"

Delphine put out a little sign on the door with an adjustable clock hand that said she would be back at two p.m. She took note of Lilith hovering nearby.

"It's about time."

"Patience," Delphine responded. "She is almost there."

The sandy beach was littered with red and white umbrellas and a rainbow of striped lawn chairs that were easily obtained from one of the local rental stands. The beach crowd was not as large as it would be on the weekends, but there was still a joyful buzz in the air, typical of children who are free from the classroom and adults untethered from their offices.

Margo and Delphine made their way to the waves in diametrically opposed states of anticipation. Delphine was more than happy to welcome Margo into the fold. Margo wanted to be reassured that she was the victim of hallucinations. Perhaps she should have gone to see the doctor instead of Delphine.

"What I tell you should be held in strict confidence, at least, for now. Even your nearest and dearest would be overwhelmed by it. Inside you beats the heart of the most powerful witch Oyster Cove has ever seen. Possibly the most powerful in all of New England."

"Hah, east of the Mississippi is more like," Lilith sneered proudly.

Delphine examined Margo's shock. "Her abilities exceeded my own by a mile. I am heavily reliant on enhancers and conductors—those would be amulets, talismans, wands, and familiars. Those are items that concentrate one's power, much like a magnifying glass. Lilith was so powerful, she seldom needed them. And while most of us are limited to proximity magic, Lilith could cause great consequences at significant distances. Her body was the only enhancement she needed. Her power coursed through her veins, burst out of every pore, and was contained in every molecule of her body, every organ. Power so potent, it has outlived her.

You have her heart, Margo, and all the power it contained has taken root in you. I sensed it that day in her home. It was irrefutable. You were one of us. You *are* one of us."

Margo pulled away. "I'm not a witch. That's impossible."

"Then why did you come to see me? Something happened. Something you couldn't explain? In a moment of anger, perhaps?"

Margo looked at her wide-eyed, not even wanting to confirm.

"Anger does not need to be feared or suppressed. It is like fuel. I'm sure it was the driving force behind Lilith's power."

"That doesn't sound very nice," Margo said miserably.

Delphine chuckled. "I don't think that anyone ever accused Lilith of being nice."

"Hey, hey, hey." Lilith bristled.

Delphine shrugged. "It's true."

"But that is not the standard she is to be judged by. Lilith was a force of nature," Delphine continued.

"You were friends?"

"No. Although . . . I wouldn't have minded that. I'm sure I could have learned a great deal from her. I don't know if I had anything equivalent to offer . . . except for my crab cakes. They are divine, if I do say so myself."

Lilith was taken aback. She was certain the other witches in town regarded her with fear and jealousy. Hmmph!

"But, but . . . I don't want to be a witch."

"Why ever not? That's the silliest thing I ever heard. Who would renounce their natural abilities? Do people who are scientifically brilliant or athletically gifted wish that their abilities would vanish? Witches aren't bound by the limited comprehension and powers of commoners. Oh, that is how people outside our community are usually referred to. A bit derogatory, I'm afraid, but descriptive. Why choose to become one? To be fenced in by gravity and physics and the paltry reach of your six senses? Why would you want to be less than powerful?"

"But . . . what do witches do with all that power? What did Lilith Hazelwood do?"

"Anything she wanted. Surely, you can think of things that you want for yourself, your family, and your friends. Life beyond the limits of your imagination. I can help teach you everything I know."

"Are you a powerful witch?"

"Average, which is plenty."

"Maybe you can help me. I'm having trouble understanding how to find the truth and help out a friend. If he's innocent, then he needs my help, and if he's not, then I just need to be sure."

"Is this important to you?"

Margo nods.

"Good. I can think of no more perfect motive to uncover and develop your powers. Afterward, you will be in a far better position to decide whether you want to be a witch."

"It's not a decision," Lilith fumed. *"You can't decide not to be a witch!"*

"That she must discover for herself."

"Make haste, Delphine. I grow impatient."

Threats were second nature to Lilith. Delphine thought it better not to remind her that her capacity for retaliation wasn't what it used to be.

Witchcraft. Powers. Exploding glass. It was a dilemma that Margo would have to hold at arm's length. It sounded like a road from which she would never be able to turn back. When it came to Russell and the murder, perhaps she would find the answers she needed without the need to pursue these alarming new powers. Perhaps she could find all the answers she needed to find—everything, in fact, that she wanted in life—without being dragged into this strange new world.

No time like the present. If someone else had committed the murder, then they had been at the restaurant that night. How to find out who had been there? She couldn't ask Russell. If guilty, he would lie to her. If innocent, he was obviously clueless or he would have mentioned the suspect. The police were unlikely to share information with her. It was time to go to the restaurant and see what she could find out.

*****

It was the first time Margo had ever seen it. *Barcelona* was a beautiful place, Mediterranean-style with the pink adobe covering and burgundy shutters and canvases. There was patio seating at either side of the entrance and a large area to the side. At full capacity, it could hold quite a crowd.

But there was no crowd there today, although the place was clearly open, and it should have been a busy lunch hour. Margo peeked in to look about for customers in a place with about sixty booths and tables. Without the distraction of customers, it was easier to see the striking Gaudi tribute inside, with photos and colorful murals of the revolutionary artist's otherworldly work on every wall.

A young woman who looked frazzled and unhappy came to seat her.

"Welcome. Table for one?"

There was something about her that hinted this wasn't really her regular job.

"I'm Margo, a friend of Russell's."

"Oh, thank you so much for supporting us in this difficult time. It's been impossible to get customers to come in with all these terrible lies flying around, you know, poison in a restaurant."

"I believe that part was true," Margo reminded her gently.

"Well, yes . . . but Russell didn't have anything to do with it," the woman said emphatically.

"And you are . . .?"

"His fiancée. Wendy Phillips. We were planning on getting married in November. You know, when the season's over. Everything was going so well. The opening was incredible. The place was packed every night. And the food is amazing, you know. Everyone seemed to think so."

"And you work here with him?"

"No, not usually. I just do the office stuff—inventory, payroll. Russell was the chef, the visionary. This place was his beautiful dream."

Margo thought about the pride she took in her own business. What a great life Russell had created for himself. And what a mess it had become.

"Wendy, I need to talk to everyone who was working that night. Do you have that information?"

"Sure. But why?"

Margo shrugged. "Just wondering if the police missed anything."

Wendy scoffed. "After they found the arsenic, they acted like there was nothing else to look for."

"I don't want to get your hopes up."

"Thank you for even trying."

Margo took a seat in the corner table. One by one, the employees came to speak with her. Some had to be summoned from their homes since so few were needed to attend to the reduced clientele. But it was not an unpleasant wait for Margo. Wendy was so grateful, that she kept a steady supply of tapas headed in Margo's direction, who was more than happy to sample the garlic prawns, the mushroom and Gruyere quiche, and the spicy potato wedges.

Everyone seemed anxious to be helpful. Ten waiters and waitresses. Three sous chefs. Two hostesses. Margo was slowly able to piece together who had been there and when they might have had the opportunity to commit the crime.

"I know there must've been a lot of tourists, a lot of unfamiliar faces. Did anyone stand out?"

"His brother was there. I don't know why. The two of them don't get along. Ian Fowler was also here. Geez, guess he had to see with his own eyes. He owns the Italian place right across the street, *Verona*, and apparently, his own business took quite a hit after our place opened. He went inside the kitchen to complain about our customers taking up his parking spaces. You know, petty stuff."

"That Fiona Skretting. You know, the one they say is a witch."

Margo squirmed uncomfortably "You're kidding. She was here? Why?"

"Chowing down on the Thai peanut sliders and green chili and cheese tamales. It was the first and only time I've ever seen her here. People say she's one of the witches. But you probably don't believe in that kind of thing."

"What did she . . . what was she like?"

"Creepy. After the guy was poisoned, everyone was waiting for the ambulance, and everyone was horrified, right? She looked . . ."

"Indifferent?"

"Entertained."

"It was such a terrible thing for his whole family—his brother, cousin and his wife, his aunt. They were in such a loud, happy mood."

"See, the dead guy never left his seat. But I think the other two men stepped into the kitchen. They said they wanted to give their compliments to the chef. But that was before they even got their meals."

Margo knew the two men were probably just conducting loan shark business and reminding Russell that his payment was coming up real soon.

"Okay, I don't know if anyone's pointing any fingers at me, but Russell and I had a little argument that night. I lost track of one of the orders, and Russell was ticked off because it's happened before. He took me out in the alley to chew me out. At least he didn't do things like that in front of the whole crew."

"So, he was out of the kitchen for how long?"

"Three or four minutes."

"And where was his coat? Could you show me?"

The location of employee outerwear was unfortunately along the wall of the hallway to the kitchen. Very accessible to anyone going in or out.

Margo finally wound up the interviews and made her exit. She couldn't help but notice the bustling activity and crowded patio space of the Italian place across the street. Looked like Ian Fowler had managed to get his customers back. She really was going to need to have a word with him. But this whole thing was daunting. So many people, so much opportunity to tamper with the food in the coat, such weird, inexplicable behavior—okay, primarily from Fiona Skretting—just no clear answers. Margo sighed loudly in frustration. She had run right into the wall of her limitations. What might she be able to accomplish if she had those . . . powers? And what would it mean to live her life as a witch?

*****

Delphine was happy to delay opening her shop this morning in order to give Margo some personal guidance. She was only relieved that Margo seemed open to the idea that this truly was the path for her to become something better.

It was best that the lesson be conducted in a place of peace and familiarity to Margo. Thankfully, Bette went to an exercise class three times a week, right after she got off work, ensuring all the privacy they needed.

"Start with the essentials," Lilith commanded. "Teach her Refractere."

Newhart, who was in his carrier, growled frantically.

"Newhart, what's the matter with you?"

"He can feel Lilith's presence, which is a promising sign. He may make a decent familiar one day."

"Lilith's presence? She's . . . here?"

"She takes a great interest in your well-being and your entry into our community."

"You can see her? And hear her?"

"Yes. But that is a talent you are unlikely to develop. At any rate, she had requested that you learn the incantation *Refractere*. It allows you to . . . break things."

"What?"

"Much like that afternoon when you shattered your dinnerware and glass—that was fueled by emotion. But the same thing can be accomplished with this incantation and that pendant around your neck. Yes, in the hands of a commoner, it's just a pretty trinket. But in the hands of a witch, it's a very strong enhancement." Delphine looked around mischievously. "You have a lovely little home. Let's break something."

"Oh, well, I have a mug in the kitchen that's already chipped. I won't mind if that gets broken."

After Margo returned with the mug, she shook her head. "Why am I learning how to break things? That doesn't seem like a very useful skill. I mean, any toddler can break things. It would be so much cooler to be able to put things back together."

"Agreed. But it's far, far easier to do damage than to resurrect. It is one of the easiest of incantations—that is all. Not to mention, Lilith had an undeniable talent for destruction. You will come to excel at some of those abilities. Now clasp the pendant in your hand. Close your eyes. And see this mug explode. See it as vividly as you can. You'll feel the pendant getting warm in your hand. When you can see the image clearly, say *Refractere*. Repeat it until the cup shatters."

Margo did as told. She did, indeed, feel the pendant become warm in her hand, unnaturally warm. The shattering of the mug was easy to envision since she was able to draw on the nightmare incident she had caused at the pub. "*Refractere. Refractere. Refractere.*" She heard the unmistakable crash of glass breaking, and her eyes flew open.

"I told you this was an easy one. Deceptively easy, for your power is not yet strong enough to create a permanent disturbance. In other words, this cup will become whole again in about fifteen minutes, at most."

"Really? That's pretty exciting," Margo responded.

"I'm glad you think so. However, you need to be aware that it's not the goal. The goal, eventually, is to create changes and manipulations that stay put. And the stronger you become, the more capable you will be in forcing those lasting changes."

"But will I be able to put things back together, to fix things that are broken on purpose?"

"Absolutely. But it is a far more advanced skill. Baby steps."

Margo had built up a great deal of patience and discipline over her lifetime—survival necessities. But the clock was ticking for Russell. She could only hope that she could advance quickly enough to be of use to him before it was too late

.

CHAPTER SEVEN

The next morning, Margo could not help but admire herself in the mirror. No longer pale and tired, and no longer depressed. Now, the image she saw before her was bursting with health, the best possible self that she could have wished for.

The doom hanging over her existence had been replaced by a big question mark. When she knew there was no future for her, there had been no need to think about what was coming next. No need to make plans. Now that the future stretched out before her in a long, brilliantly endless fashion, what exactly *were* her plans? What was she going to do with her life?

Of course, she would always have *Margo's Movie House*. That was such an essential part of her life. There shouldn't be anything fundamentally incompatible between owning a business and being a witch. Certainly, Delphine didn't seem to have a problem with that.

Her next lesson with Delphine continued that morning, privacy assured with Bette thankfully, meeting a friend for brunch.

"Do witches all have jobs and businesses and go grocery shopping and get married? Are they like normal people? Because you seem pretty normal. But what I'm hearing about Lilith sounds like a bit of an unusual case."

"On the surface, our lives are quite ordinary. In the best of ways. I love having my own business and making jewelry. And having such a huge tourist crowd pour in every summer. And I love to go boating on the ocean. I love good food . . . but don't we all? But your experience of all these things will be enhanced to a remarkable degree. You will soon feel as if you were sleepwalking through a great deal of your life."

"And even after I learn how to be a witch, how to make things . . . happen, I still have the option of not using those abilities. Right?"

"That's nonsense," Lilith railed. "It's like an able-bodied person deciding that they don't feel like walking. Like they're just going to stop walking one day even though they can. The powers demand to be used. One might as well wrap a blindfold around one's eyes and decide to get through life without sight. Tell her, Delphine, that she has been given a great gift. I'll not have her take it lightly."

"She already treasures her newfound health and the loss of her old hesitance and timidity. It won't take long for her to appreciate the other ways in which her life has been transformed. She needs to see the benefits for herself. And as we both know, power can be downright addictive."

"Continue the lesson," Lilith ordered sternly. *"I tire of these delays."*

"Let us try *Refractere* again. The more you practice, the faster you will progress."

Margo thought that she had mastered it. She broke the glass again with little difficulty. But what Delphine wanted to see was how long the glass remained broken. Last time, it lasted for twenty minutes. This time, it reassembled after some fifteen minutes, which, again, Margo thought was the coolest part of the whole process.

"One day, you will shatter something, and it will remain so."

"What else are you going to teach me?"

"She must learn how to defend herself. Enemies are all about. We must teach her some serious defensive maneuvers."

"There's no need to alarm her. And no reason to assume that whoever targeted you will be of any danger to her. Not having your great strength, she won't pose the same threat to them."

Lilith scowled. "You lose sight of my mission. I intend to make use of this girl. Who is that? There are people approaching. Get rid of them."

"I see them. But her life must continue. Especially after it was suspended for so long. Don't worry, Lilith. I see a great future for her."

There was a knock at the door.

"Who could that be?" Margo wondered. "Sorry. I'm sure this'll just be a minute."

She opened the front door and was stunned to see Finn Cochran, a.k.a. 'Mark Ruffalo' or 'Mr. Lethal Weapon' and a young girl at his side who looked to be about twelve years old.

With her dark pixie haircut, she reminded Margo of a tweeny Winona Ryder.

"Good morning. Sorry to just drop in like this without any notice. I just wanted to say that I'm sorry for being such a jerk the other night at the beach. My name's Finn in case you forgot. You're Margo Bailey. And this here is my niece, Zoe Larson."

"Hi," Zoe chirped cheerfully. She examined Margo with undisguised enthusiasm.

"Uh, hi. Nice to meet you."

Margo glanced behind her, not certain if Delphine would tolerate strangers intruding on their clandestine little lesson, but Delphine was *gone*.

"So I brought Zoe here to offer her services as a token of my apology."

"Services?"

Zoe backed away from the steps and onto the front yard, where she threw up her arms and executed a perfect cartwheel. Margo gasped in amazement.

"As you know, I am cartwheel challenged. But Zoe here will hook you up. She's taught this to other friends. Go ahead. Give her a try."

It was such a crazy little thing to be fixated on. Margo had always wanted to do a cartwheel. This was a pretty bizarre turn of events. What did he say his name was? Finn? And he had dragged his niece here? How did he even know where she lived? But there wasn't a whole lot of time to figure things out. Zoe was dragging her into the middle the yard, ready to begin their lessons.

"Uncle Finn, come over here. You stand right behind her and if it looks like she's about to fall over, give her legs a push forward. Just make sure she doesn't kick you in the face."

"Uh, I was just gonna watch. I had no idea my face was going to be involved in any way or I would've brought a helmet."

Margo actually turned out to be a quick study. So much so that Finn's backup assistance was dispensed with after ten minutes, whereupon he returned to the front porch and was happy to watch from a distance. He couldn't help but smile at how clearly delighted that Margo was to check this high-priority item from her bucket list. It had been a long time since he had seen anyone so full of unmitigated joy. The fact that that joy was wrapped in an alluring, adorable package was not lost on him.

Despite giving her full attention to the cartwheel lesson, Margo could not help but be aware of Finn's eyes on her. She couldn't even recall giving him her name that night on the beach. Of course! He must've gotten it from the police guest log, where she signed in with her address as well. But this was a pretty extreme measure, to track her down. Sure, he behaved like a jerk but, why would he be so bothered by it to go to such lengths to apologize? And to bring his niece! The motivation was so obvious, so glaring, that her cheeks slowly flushed. He wanted to get to know her.

Margo and Zoe finally approached Finn on the porch.

"Very nice. Cirque du Soleil, here we come," Finn teased.

"I am going to dazzle my sister and make her very jealous," Margo declared with a big grin. Her latest talent acquisition clearly couldn't hold a candle to acquiring magical powers. But she was still well aware that she had her new heart to thank for this surreal moment.

"Say, it's gonna be a scorcher today. Maybe you'd like to join me and Zoe and take a little dip at the beach," Finn said, trying to sound nonchalant.

"Yeah, Margo, say yes, say yes, say yes, say yes," Zoe pleaded.

"That's very nice, but . . . this is going to sound silly. I haven't been swimming since my lessons in high school. I don't even have a swimming suit."

"You live in Oyster Cove. You live in a beach town. And you have no swimming suit?" Finn asked incredulously.

"Whenever I needed to cool off, I just waded in up to my knees. I know how to swim. I just *don't* swim."

"There's a ton of sales on swimsuits right now," Zoe said. "We passed a bunch of them. Really cheap. It's a good time to buy one. I'll help you. You try them on and I'll let you know which one looks the best."

"I, too, would like to offer my services," Finn said, trying to keep a straight face. "If you want to try on swimsuits, I'd be happy to offer my humble opinion."

"Don't be a doofus, Uncle Finn. You can go off and do something while I give her a hand. And then we can meet up afterward and go to the beach. Okay, Margo? How does that sound?"

"I have to be at work by 3:45 p.m.," Margo said, mind spinning.

"Okay, shopping first, then a couple of hours on the beach, then we can get lunch somewhere," Zoe decided. "His treat."

"Very generous of me," Finn teased. "No, absolutely. Please join us for lunch. That's part two of the apology."

"What's part three?" Zoe wondered.

Finn looked away with a little embarrassed smile. Perhaps part three was a little too PG-13.

*****

It had been a long time since Margo had spent time with such a young girl. And she couldn't remember when the last time was when she had met anyone who was so determined to be her friend. At least, not including Zoe's uncle.

There were three dressing room stalls, but they were the only customers around. Zoe stood outside the door and ferried swimsuits back and forth, getting new sizes and putting the rejects back.

"So, your uncle seems like a pretty cool guy," Margo said nonchalantly.

"He's super cool—we're all so glad that he's okay. He was in the hospital for two months. The first two weeks, in an induced coma. That had us all freaking out. But it was to stabilize him. I've never been so scared in my life. But he looks good now, right?"

"That's horrible. And wonderful that he's so well now."

"Well, we're happy he got this job in Oyster Cove. He always used to have to travel so much. He didn't get a chance to see his family that much. No chance to have a real girlfriend." She looked meaningfully at Margo.

"You do realize that your uncle and I barely know each other. In fact, we *don't* know each other. I don't know anything about him."

"What do you want to know?"

Margo paused to think. Another unprecedented opportunity. They seemed to be popping up all over the place. "What do you like most about him?"

"Okay, so when I was young—okay, okay, younger—I broke one of my mother's favorite Christmas bulbs. Uncle Finn was visiting, and he told her he had done it. Afterward, he told me, in general, that it's not okay to lie, blah, blah, blah. But after that, I knew he would always look out for me."

So, Mr. Lethal Weapon was a nice guy. Six months ago, she would have shied away from the thought of getting close to him because of her weak heart and bleak future. Now, she had to wonder what on earth he would think if he were aware of the whole witch thing? She absentmindedly stepped out of the dressing stall wearing a red and white striped bikini, probably the tenth suit she had tried on.

"Winner!" Zoe declared jubilantly.

Margo smiled. Was this what it would've been like to have a little sister?

*****

The water was bracingly cold. Margo squealed as the icy water crashed over her. Five minutes was all it took for their bodies to acclimate. Zoe accelerated the process by splashing as much water as she could on the other two. Margo was glad that the others were unaware that completely immersing herself in cold water had been on her taboo list. It was a blueprint for a heart attack. Now, the playful waves felt like yet another new friend.

When Margo and Finn stopped for little break, Zoe stayed in, purposefully giving the other two a little alone time. A cheerful fellow with an icy beverage cart rolled right up to them.

"Icy cold sparklers. Just the thing to hit the spot."

"Let me see. Hmm. Pineapple coconut. Raspberry kiwi. Guava passion fruit. That's the ticket. What do you think?" Finn asked Margo.

"That doesn't sound bad."

"We'll take three."

Margo accepted the drink gratefully. She looked around at the crowded beach and smiled. "I feel like a tourist today. I feel like I'm on vacation."

Finn tried to restrain an admiring glance, not altogether successfully. "You look like a tourist."

"Yeah? Well, you look like . . . like . . ." Margo was finally able to indulge her inclination to examine her bare-chested companion. There was much to admire. The man stayed fit. But there was also . . .

"Is that a . . .a . . .?"

"A bullet hole?" Finn offered helpfully. "Yeah, it sure is. I've got five of them. Want to see the others?"

Margo was about to retort that she had no interest in his other wounds. Except that she did. What a terrible thing to have happened to him. Suddenly, she really needed to know what he had been through. The first bullet had caught him on the right side of his waist. The second was to his shoulder.

"My aim was a little wobbly after that one," Finn commented. "A lot of physical therapy on that one."

The next went through his left hand. The fourth, through his upper right arm. Margo searched vainly for the fifth bullet hole.

"I know what you're thinking. You're thinking, gluteus maximus. I'm right, aren't I? You're thinking about my gluteus maximus?"

"I am not thinking about your . . . that is not where you got shot. Is it? Oh, no. Is that where the fifth bullet hole is?"

Finn shrugged tragically. Then his face popped into a grin. "I should probably have left you in suspense. But here you go."

He bent his head down close to her and brushed his hair back with his hand. There it was, a bullet hole right above his left ear, right through his skull. Margo felt sick.

"That's actually holes five and six, but they were made by the same bullet," Finn explained. "No, don't look like that. That's all behind me. I'm doing just great now."

"That's why you were in the hospital for two months," Margo said.

"That Zoe . . . biggest mouth in the family. Yeah, two months. And the family nagged me to get a new job. I still don't know if that was the right move. But I needed a little time to think, so . . . Oyster Cove. Close to the family. But not too close, you know what I'm sayin'? Chance to get some surfing in before I forget how.

"Surfing!"

"That's right. This cartwheel challenged boy can surf. Hey, Zoe should probably come in."

Margo looked out at the swimming area. It was cordoned off on three sides with the buoy line and the lifeguard's station right at the edge. Zoe was bobbing up and down the far corner. Close enough to the line for safety. But, still . . .

"Let's go get her," she said enthusiastically, running for the water.

"But you can't swim!" Finn yelled, close on her heels.

"'Course I could swim. I swam two full laps across the pool once. Just never in the ocean. And not recently. But of course I remember how to do it. Everyone can do it, so why shouldn't I be able to?"

She plunged into the water, taking in the sensation of being tossed about by the waves in an amused and detached manner. Instinctively, just as she had known her heart could handle the ladder, and could handle a full out sprint around the hospital, she knew her heart could conquer the ocean. Not just the endurance involved, but the fear.

There was no panicking. She made her way confidently toward the corner where Zoe was hanging out and felt a thrill when she knew that she had gone so far, there was no more touching the ground. Wow! She had a heart sturdier than her wildest dreams. She and Finn reached Zoe at about the same time.

"Okay, both of you come in before you give me a heart attack," Finn demanded.

"Only if you promise—" Margo began.

"I promise. I promise. What am I promising?"

"You're going to teach me how to surf," Margo crowed. Among the many new sensations she'd experienced over the last few weeks, that of having a man wrapped around her finger was a truly astonishing development. And for a month where she had acquired a new heart and discovered witchly powers, that was really saying something.

CHAPTER EIGHT

There was a freestanding surf supply shack just about fifty yards in from the waves. Margo had walked past it hundreds of times, taking little notice of it. What was she ever going to have to do with surfing? And now here she was, in a wetsuit, with a long, heavy surfboard under her arm.

"Already looking like a pro," Finn said admiringly.

He cut quite the figure himself. Who knew rubber could be so sexy?

"Okay. First thing is to learn how to get on the board."

Margo thought for a second and then quickly stepped on the board planted on the sand in front of her and looked toward Finn for the next step.

"Oh, a regular prodigy. That move can come very handy if you can walk on water. Can you walk on water?"

Could she? "Not that I know of."

"How about we try this lying on the board . . . that's right. Now, you pop up in as close to a single motion as possible and land right in the middle. Stick that landing like a gold medal gymnast."

Perhaps it was her recent practice with cartwheels. Margo's unshakable faith that all things were now within grasp had her leaping confidently up and landing firmly.

Finn assured her that the most difficult part of her day was going to be not panicking and recovering after each spill, of which there would be many. Margo had already conquered her fear of deep waves the previous day. All that seemed required was an attitude adjustment. Expect to fall. Enjoy the fall. Play with the fall. The friendly waters would always carry her back to the surface.

Finn was amazed. "Man, you can handle anything. I've never seen anyone so relaxed the first time out."

"Well, it must be because I have such a talented instructor."

"If you had such a talented instructor, you wouldn't keep falling off."

Margo pretended to be affronted.

"No, I mean, you've got something you can't bottle, sell, or buy. No fear—it's very unusual. Were you born that way?"

"Aren't we all?"

Finn shook his head. He'd never met anyone like her.

"I'm not going to stop until I make at least one ride all the way in," Margo declared.

"All right, let's see it."

As it so happened, Margo was able to complete three rides into shore without losing her balance. It was like flying! The final ride came with an unforgettable surprise. While she and Finn were waiting for the right wave, a dolphin started circling them.

"Ooh! Hello there. Aren't you the friendly one? Come here."

The dolphin swam right up against Margo's outstretched hand. Finn held his breath as the dolphin poked its head onto Margo's board. She gently rubbed its head, which it seemed to enjoy. It looked Margo right in the eye as she murmured gently, admiring its beauty and bravery. After a few moments, it slipped back into the water below. Finn knew what Margo was thinking.

"No. That never happens. Never, never, ever, never. You're thinking, oh yeah, the dolphin stopped by to say hello. Trust me. That never happens."

"I think dolphins are just more sociable than you realized. Oh, here's our wave."

Finn watched Margo take yet another successful ride back to shore. Her balance was fantastic. There was something more about her than natural athleticism. What was up with that dolphin?

Margo wondered the same thing herself. Maybe the dolphins had some natural chemistry with witches. More importantly, where was the chemistry with this young cop going to lead?

*****

Though life was increasingly full of distractions, Margo had to maintain her focus on getting to the bottom of Julian Meeks's murder. She knew that she had to speak to everyone of note who had gone to the restaurant that night. She roped Bette into having a late lunch at *Verona*, the Italian eatery across from Russell's tapas restaurant.

Even though it was the end of lunch hour, the place was still pretty crowded. It seemed that the stain on *Barcelona* had driven customers right back to *Verona*. Things were so busy that they had to take a buzzer and sit in a waiting area until a table was ready for them. The restaurant was clean and tastefully decorated, but nondescript, with none of the creative effort that Russell had poured into his tapas place.

"Okay, so the plan is, we have lunch and then I get lost?" Bette asked.

"That's the plan. I need to talk to this owner, Ian Fowler. It's probably nothing, but just to be sure."

"Whatever. But let's get to the important matter. Finn Cochran. Tell me everything."

"I already did tell you everything. There's just not a whole lot to tell."

"It's like pulling teeth. Okay, how old is he?"

"I didn't ask. He looked a bit older than me."

"Who would play him?"

"A young Mark Ruffalo . . . and pretty fit."

"That's so unfair! I love Mark Ruffalo a lot more than you do."

"Mark Ruffalo only exists in the movies. This guy is . . . very real. For some reason, we seem to get along."

"You're killing me. And you said government law enforcement. What agency?"

"I didn't ask."

"You're useless."

"He's a very sweet uncle. He knows how to surf. And he likes horror movies."

"He sounds like a prince. Can't wait to meet him."

Their buzzer finally rang. They both ordered the shrimp ravioli special, which smelled heavenly and tasted pretty great. They also had a really tasty side of fried calamari, which Margo didn't mind sharing with Newhart, who waited impatiently below the table in his carrier. The meal was a bit pricey, but it was definitely targeting the tourist crowd. Margo asked the waitress if she could have word with the owner, assuring her that the service had been terrific, and Bette made a quick exit.

Ian Fowler came straight to her table, looking concerned.

"Everything okay, ma'am?"

"Everything was terrific. That shrimp ravioli was spectacular. I'm going to have to tell all my friends about it."

"That's nice to hear. That's really nice to hear. So, how can I help you?"

"I'm Margo Bailey. I own *Margo's Movie House.*"

"All right. Yeah, yeah. I hear it's a great place. 'Course, running the restaurant in the evenings, I can never get to the movies."

"Well, I just had an idea to run past you. I belong to an association of small businesses and we meet monthly. It's the whole Cape Cod area. And they're a great bunch of people. But as business owners in Oyster Cove, we don't have exactly the same issues and concerns as Martha's Vineyard. Am I right?"

"Yeah, I see what you're sayin'."

"So I'm putting together a local business association, and I wanted to talk to local owners and just figure out what our big issues are, how we might be able to help one another, what legislation we should be pressing for, and, you know, what's going to make Oyster Cove a better place to conduct business. Do you have any time right now? Just twenty minutes in your office would be great."

"Sure, that sounds good. Yeah, there's a bunch of things I can think of to improve things for people like us."

Ian's office was a modest size, filled with do-it-yourself IKEA-style furniture and one tall metal file cabinet. It looked as if he'd just been working on his desktop computer.

"Your business is doing so well. I was worried that the poisoning at Russell Knox's restaurant might've scared the tourists away. You know how irrational people can be."

Ian shook his head sadly. "Shame. Terrible shame. I'm still kind of in shock over it. And it does shake the customers' faith in the people who serve them. I gotta admit I felt a little bit betrayed. I was like his mentor. Showed him the ropes, gave him advice on where to get the good equipment, taught him about the regulations, how to fill out the permits . . ."

"Well, you got him off to a great start. *Barcelona* was going like gangbusters for a while there."

"Yeah, who'd have thunk? I honestly didn't figure there'd be that much of a demand for little hors d'oeuvres. Guess it was a novelty thing. Yeah, he was pulling quite a crowd. Of course, the guy has to close up now. Terrible."

"That just reminded me. That place will need a new renter. You know who it would be perfect for? This guy in Provincetown who's got this crazy popular barbecue joint, and he was looking for a second location. We don't have anything like that in Oyster Cove yet. And you know how the summer crowd loves barbecue. He would clean up."

"Now hold on. That's not a very good idea. In fact, that's a terrible idea. You can't be putting these restaurants too close together. They need to be spread out, for everyone's sake. I mean, you wouldn't want to have three fish and chips places on the same block, right?"

"No, not the same type of food. You're right about that. But different kinds of food . . ."

"Better for businesses to have, you know, a complementary symbiotic relationship, you know what I'm saying? Like a hotel. The people stay there and then cross the street to my place for dinner. Or like a dance club. The people dance for hours, work up an appetite, and then come over to my place for a little snack. Businesses that help each other out. You know what I'm saying?"

Mighty convenient for you that Russell is out of business. The question is did you have anything to do with it? "I'm sorry to bother you, but could you bring me a little bowl of water for my cat? I think he's getting a little dehydrated."

"Sure, sure. No problem. Back in a sec."

As soon as he had closed the door to the office, Margo clasped her pendant and pointed at the door lock. "*Refractere*," she said decisively. Then she tested the door—it wouldn't open. It was jammed—it worked! Then she turned her attention to the desktop computer. She'd have to wrestle with her ethics later. Right now, she needed to search that browser history and find out whether there were any searches for arsenic or food poisoning. Or any mention of Russell Knox.

Indeed, there were a few searches on arsenic. But they all seemed to occur after Russell's arrest date. Just another member of the public interested in a scintillating news story. Also a search on Russell's business. Real estate searches. And what was this? Food poisoning searches. A whole bunch of them. Dating back a few weeks, and certainly predating the murder. Why? Was it about an issue that came up at his own restaurant?

What had she been thinking? Even if Ian were behind this, he wouldn't be stupid enough to leave evidence lying about. But not being able to prove something is not the same thing as disproving it. She couldn't shake the feeling that Ian Fowler was up to no good. She certainly couldn't be dissuaded by the delectable ravioli.

The door handle rattled.

"Hey! What's going on?"

"What you mean?" Margo asked innocently.

"Door's locked. Did you do that?"

Margo walked over to the door and tried to open it. It was still jammed.

"The lock's not working. Don't you have a key?"

"I sure do."

She heard the key slip into the lock and his angry, frustrated groans is it failed to open the door.

"What the heck? What did you do?"

"I haven't touched it except to try to open it just now when you asked me to. It sounds very defective." Margo flinched. Lying did not come easily to her.

"For heaven sake. Gonna have to take off the hinges. I can't believe this. You hold tight—back in a minute."

Margo proceeded to rifle through the metal file cabinet. It looked identical to pretty much all other small business folders that you expect to find. Health permits, state regs, employee files, liquor license folder . . . which reminded her she'd have to check on her petition at the liquor board again soon. The customers loved the BYOB option in her two small parlor-like viewing rooms. But it would be much nicer if she could stock bottles of wine for sale. She had been waiting patiently for a response from her petition. But Russell's paperwork had gotten messed up. Maybe hers had been as well.

But a quick check in the liquor license folder revealed two envelopes that definitely looked as if they didn't belong in Ian Fowler's file cabinet—as they were addressed to Russell Knox! A quick look inside revealed letters from the liquor bureau that said that his application had been incorrectly filled out and that he would have to revise it and resubmit.

But Russell had never seen these documents. He had waited and waited, and finally contacted the Bureau, and assumed that they had messed up their jobs. And then he did resubmit, and waited and waited some more. And while he was waiting, he was unable to open his restaurant, and eventually, was unable to pay Julian Meeks back on the loan. Ian Fowler had created all that trouble for Russell. Whether he was involved in framing him for murder, she couldn't say. But this was bad enough. This was infuriating. She tucked the letters inside her purse.

Through the door, she could hear Ian muttering and grumbling.

"This is crazy. Sure you didn't touch the lock? "

"Never laid a hand on it."

Margo wondered how long it would take for the lock to unbreak. As luck would have it, it was still inexplicably broken ten minutes later when Ian was able to unscrew the hinges off. He opened it and suspiciously examined the derelict doorknob. Margo scooped up Newhart's carrier.

"Litter box time. Gotta go."

"I thought you might have some more questions for me."

"No, you gave me a lot to think about. Support. Mentoring. Symbiotic relationships."

With a big, fake, grateful smile plastered on her face, Margo made her exit. Walking home, she sighed, disappointed. She knew more than she had before, but nothing about the murder.

Again bumping up against her frustrating limitations, Margo eagerly looked forward to the next lesson with Delphine. Perhaps she would learn how to read minds or see shadows of the past. Or speak to Julian Meeks's ghost—something that would be useful for solving this case.

She also thought that it was about time that she discussed the case with someone who actually solved murders for a living. Good thing she had a date with one tonight.

*****

Margo and Finn had just come out of the last showing of *Casablanca* at her theater and headed over to *The Clam Shack* next door. The walls and corners of the eatery were crammed with hanging fishnets, anchors, buoys, ship models . . . over the top nautical excess that tourists and locals alike got a kick out of.

Margo tried to ignore Clarissa's big, curious eyes and gestures in Finn's direction.

"It's on the house. Whatever you want, my pleasure," Clarissa gushed.

"You don't have to do that," Margo protested.

"You let me sneak into movies for free all the time. And since I will continue to do so, I think I can spare a few clams."

"All right then, I'll take this scallop special. How about you?" She asked Finn.

"The crab sticks sound really good," Finn said.

"That'll just be ten minutes," Clarissa said.

"You must be a real VIP," Finn said. "Gettin' meals comped like a boss."

She knew that he was teasing. But just being on a date with this very hot guy who couldn't take his eyes off her went a long way toward making her feel like a VIP.

"So, how did you like the movie this time around?"

"I can't believe it was the same movie that I saw when I was sixteen. All I can remember is thinking that Humphrey Bogart wasn't a terribly good-looking guy. And his character wasn't even very nice. But yet this woman, this gorgeous woman, was crazy about him. And then the end left me a little befuddled. Because if you're lucky enough to have a woman like that love you, you just hold on for dear life."

"This time, I'm hoping it made a better impression."

"Well, I finally noticed all that political stuff that you said to look out for. American isolationist policy before World War II, and Rick standing in for that. And then eventually, Rick and America making sacrifices for the greater good. That just completely went over my head when I was sixteen and probably would have again if you hadn't told me to look out for it."

"It's nothing original, I assure you. I read a lot of movie critiques. But it's just so well done. And the dialogue is just the best."

"I have to hand it to you. You know how to pick 'em. But you've promised—next time, I get to introduce you to my taste in movies. And you'll keep an open mind, right?"

"Does any of these movies you have in mind feature someone named Jason or Chucky?"

"Oh, no. That would ruin the surprise."

They exchanged a long smile, and Margo looked away thoughtfully.

"Franc for your thoughts?" Finn teased.

"I wanted to talk about Russell Knox," Margo began.

"I was afraid of that," Finn said, shaking his head. "But I'm really not allowed to discuss the details of this case."

"I didn't want you to tell me anything. I wanted to tell you something. You know Ian Fowler, the owner of the *Verona* restaurant across from Russell's place?"

"*Verona*, yeah. Great sausage lasagna."

"You've been over there? What were you doing over there? Did you try to talk to Ian?"

Finn shrugged noncommittally.

"Is Ian Fowler a suspect?" Margo asked excitedly.

"Hey, keep it down," Finn shushed her. "He's just . . . a person of interest."

Margo gingerly pulled the letters from the liquor license bureau out of her purse. "Ian Fowler stole these letters from the liquor license bureau and tried to ruin Russell Knox's business."

"Yeah? Where'd you get those letters?"

"Out of the file cabinet in Ian Fowler's office."

"I did not hear that. Are you insane?

"That's a crime all by itself, isn't it?"

"By him or by you? By him? Maybe. Maybe not. Little hard to prove now that the letters are no longer in his possession and your fingerprints are all over them."

"I actually tried to handle them very carefully. I'm sure Ian's fingerprints are still there. Can you check them?"

Finn took the letters by the corner edges. "Maybe. But I'm still not seeing a connection to the murder."

"Ian hated the competition from Russell's restaurant. He tried to slow down his liquor license, and he did, by six months. It put Russell in a bad spot. But he finally made a huge success with the restaurant, and Ian lost a big chunk of his business."

"Okay . . . what next?"

"He had to try something else to shut Russell down. Something to take away Russell's business. Scandal. A rumor. Food poisoning. What if Ian arranged the food poisoning? And maybe he didn't even intend to kill anyone, just have someone get sick at Russell's place and ruin the reputation of the restaurant. Maybe things got out of hand. He used too much arsenic. Maybe he never intended for someone to die."

"You've got imagination, I'll give you that. You know we don't get that many arsenic cases these days. Antifreeze is now the number one way for people to poison someone. Everyone's got some in the garage. Nothing suspicious about it. But arsenic . . . that's a lot harder to acquire and a lot harder to explain. Leaves a trail of some kind, one way or the other."

"What if he had access to poison? Don't restaurants use rat poison? Maybe that's how he got it."

Finn pulled out his cellphone and pulled up an arsenic webpage. "Not really used for rat poison. They're worried about kids and animals having too much access to it. But it's still used in electronics, LED lights, and wood—it prevents wood from rotting. Lotta buildings that got put up with lead in the walls also had to be checked for arsenic as well."

"Will you look into it?" Margo pleaded.

"I'll do that. But you've got to stop stealing things."

"It didn't belong to Ian Fowler. There's nothing wrong with trying to restore something to its rightful owner . . . but it sounds as if you're at least willing to entertain the possibility that Russell is not the killer."

"There's plenty of evidence against him. But there's things about his case that never added up. Why kill someone in your own restaurant and keep the poison in your car? It's not smart. Not saying that criminals are always smart, but . . . the thing that puzzles me the most is no motive. There's absolutely no reason for Russell Knox to target Julian Meeks. No motive whatsoever."

Margo shifted uncomfortably. There actually was an incredibly damning motive. Finn and the police were still unaware of the $50,000 that Russell owed Julian Meeks and was not going to be able to pay. If they did know, the following up of all other leads would come to a crashing halt. So as badly as she felt about it, Finn was going to have to be kept in the dark a bit longer about that very problematic detail.

CHAPTER NINE

Knowing how to break things was bad enough. Learning how to hurt people? Maybe she didn't want to be a witch after all.

"Why? Why? That's a terrible thing to know how to do—you want to turn me into a human taser?" Margo wailed.

Delphine shrugged apologetically. "Lilith had a special affinity for electricity. As a rule, it requires very strong anger to activate, which she could summon at will. It is a great irony that she died of a lightning strike. It was widely rumored that when there was an electrical storm about, she could redirect it toward whatever target suited her, human or otherwise."

"I don't want to hurt anyone."

"Stop being a baby," Lilith groaned. "The first order of life is to protect oneself. To be stronger than all adversaries. To fear no one."

This was a bit stronger than Delphine would have framed it. Perhaps it would help to provide some context. "Lilith's mother died shortly after her birth—like yours. But under suspicious circumstances. Lilith had to be very mindful of the dangers and enemies that surround us. She recommends that you look upon this as a self-defense class. Hopefully, you'll never need it. But if you do . . ."

Margo shook her head. "I'll be able to touch someone and zap them with electricity?"

"Well, yes. Not unlike static electricity—but with quite a bit more voltage. Of course, Lilith didn't have to be close enough to touch. She could send someone a jolt from a considerable distance. I witnessed it myself once. But again, she was formidable. It's likely you'll always have to touch whatever you are . . . zapping."

Reluctantly, Margo agreed to acquire this latest skill. Lilith's heart had given her life, and freedom, and courage. It seemed ungracious to reject all the other things that came with it.

Delphine directed Margo to keep one hand on her pendant and the other holding a sheet of paper, chanting *Nesploro Fiere*, and she gave her instructions to go to the polar opposite of her happy place. In order to summon her inner Lilith, Margo needed to get good and mad. Not as easy as it sounded.

"Have you ever had a terrible boss?" Delphine offered helpfully.

"No. I did have a few jobs before opening the theater. But they were all so sweet to me. Probably because they knew about the heart problem. My employers really looked out for me—very considerate, all of them."

"What about family? Relatives? Rivalries, disputes, backstabbing?"

"Bette is my only relative now. She's been an angel. I couldn't have made it without her."

"Exes? Nasty jerk boyfriends?"

"There weren't that many. And they weren't such bad fellows. Actually, I just met someone. We don't really know each much about each other, but . . ." Margo's mind drifted off into engrossing reveries.

It was time to get tough. "A man was killed in your friend's restaurant, and they weren't just content to kill. No, they had to make sure that another person took the fall. Right now, they've got their feet up somewhere, glass of scotch in hand, thinking what a pathetic sap your friend Russell is and not feeling a shred of guilt because Russell's life was worthless and insignificant. Disposable. They think about him in a six by ten cell. And they laugh. They are *laughing*."

Margo bristled. That was probably close enough to the truth. Someone had callously, inexcusably framed Russell for murder and was now just twiddling their thumbs, waiting for him to be tried and found guilty and given a life sentence. Whoever it was, she could just . . .

"*Nesploro Fiere! Nesploro Fiere! Nesploro Fiere!*"

The paper burst into flame. She tossed it into the nearby sink, her own eyes still ablaze with anger.

"Oh, my dear," Delphine said admiringly. "I was sure that would take you a few weeks. But you're a natural."

"I just got so mad," Margo said haltingly.

"I told you, don't fear your anger and don't suppress it. It can be channeled into power. It's true for all witches, but especially so for Lilith Hazelwood. And you have exhibited some of her most distinctive tendencies."

"I wish she had been a whiz at solving murders."

"She's thinking about that young man in jail again," Lilith groused. "It is my murder that she should turn her attention to. You must explain to her exactly what her duty is to me and that she owes her life and all of her powers to me."

"Let her strength grow first. Today was an important step. And her courage grows daily. But her ability still lags behind her courage, and there's no telling what danger that could put her in."

"Discourage all distractions," Lilith demanded.

"Why don't I walk you back to your shop?" Margo offered. "I've got to pick up a few things at the store for tonight. My new friend Finn is coming over. I think you'd like him."

Lilith's groan was so loud, it sent Newhart running for shelter.

*****

Bette was thrilled that Finn was scheduled to arrive before she had to leave for her evening shift. On the one hand, she couldn't be happier that Margo finally had a new fella in her life. At the same time, he'd better be a pretty spectacular guy. Not just any man was good enough for her little sister.

"I'll get it! I'll get it!" Bette yelled when the doorbell rang. She opened the door and could only shake her head at Margo's good fortune. Absolutely, Mark Ruffalo.

"Hi, I'm Bette. You must be Finn. Come on in."

"*Enchante*," Finn responded. Margo had advised him that he would best endear himself to Bette by showing a little continental flair. She was right. Bette looked about to swoon.

"You speak French?" Bette gushed.

"I had to go to Paris to extradite a prisoner. Picked up a few essentials."

"Cool. FBI or CIA?"

"FBI. Right out of college."

"Ooh, America's Most Wanted?"

Finn nodded modestly.

"Did you catch any?" Bette asked excitedly.

"We put a few away. I was on a good team."

"But you're retired. You're awfully young. And how young, exactly, are you?"

"Thirty-one."

"Siblings?"

"Two. Brother and a sister. Whole family still in Boston."

"Brother? Good-looking single brother?"

Finn grinned. "Yeah, he's single. It's hard for me to say if he's good-looking. He looks a lot like me."

Bette gasped. Margo shook her head at her sister's brazen lack of shame.

"And the vetting process is complete. You passed," Bette informed him.

"Isn't it time for you to get to work?" Margo scolded.

Bette didn't object—the more time these two spent alone together, the juicier the details would be afterward. She could wait. After her departure, there was one more introduction to make.

"Remember what I told you about Newhart. I know it's really difficult, but try to keep your feet away from him. He's still so skittish about that."

"I remembered. Your sister's not the only one who is going to be blown away by my charm."

Margo went to her room where she knew Newhart was luxuriating in his kitty bed. She brought him to Finn. Stroking him carefully, speaking to him softly, and preparing him for what would surely be a slightly jarring addition to his life, she set him gently on the floor.

"You just have a seat on the sofa and let him get used to the sight of you. Then when he's ready, maybe we'll put him in your lap so he doesn't have to deal with the sight of your feet."

Finn complied. "Here, kitty, kitty, kitty. Uncle Finn is here. I think you're gonna like me."

Margo had expected Newhart to turn around and run into the next room. But he was looking at Finn very curiously. He inched closer and closer and then did something most remarkable. He made a beeline for Finn's feet! He sniffed his shoes, batted them with his paws, sniffed them again, and then threw his body on top of Finn's shoes and started snuggling against them. Margo watched in amazement. Newhart backed off the feet and started batting them again with his paws. And then he stretched on them again, tummy up, arms waving furiously in the air. Finn looked triumphant.

"What is going on?" Margo asked.

"Your cat appears to be a little under the influence. I may have overdone it a bit."

"Is that . . . is that . . .? Did you put catnip on your shoes?"

Finn nodded guiltily. "How else do you make friends with a cat?"

"Not by drugging him."

"I think he likes me though."

"He's inebriated."

"Yeah, ya think he's gonna have a little kitty hangover tomorrow?"

"You ought to be ashamed."

But Margo wasn't really irritated. Even this silly bickering with Finn was all part of a dream come true. A modest dream by most people's standards, but one that she had sadly accepted would never be part of her reality. An intriguing young man was in her house, trying to impress her sister and her cat, all to ingratiate himself further with her. And they were going to spend the evening eating some homemade snacks and watching a scary movie. And who knew what else?

"What is that delectable smell?"

"Lobster quesadillas. I need to finish putting them together," Margo said. "Don't get Newhart into any more trouble."

"I will not let him drive or operate machinery in his present condition."

Margo was halfway to the kitchen when she turned. "Oh, what movie did you bring?"

"I brought something that, like *Casablanca*, is a true classic of American cinema. With timeless lessons of human endurance, courage, despair, hubris, and loyalty, a really unmatched encapsulation of the human experience."

Margo raised her eyebrows suspiciously. "Don't leave me in suspense."

"*Alien*. Ah, I can tell this is going to be your first time. More like six or seven for me. It's gonna blow you away. Guaranteed."

As a film lover, Margo wasn't sure that *Alien* should be mentioned in the same breath as *Casablanca*. But scary movies were a good test for the rapidly increasing strength of her new heart. And her regular old conventional human heart was being stretched to the limit as well. Finn was looking very good.

"We should probably eat by the half hour mark of the movie, 'cause after that, you may lose your appetite," Finn warned. "Trust me."

He turned out to be right. Margo flinched, shuddered, gasped, and peeked squeamishly through her fingers at the unspeakable monstrosity on the screen. And her heart pounded away like crazy. Who knew being scared could be this much fun?

Afterward, Finn could tell by the big grin on Margo's face that he'd made a convert. "You're a lucky, lucky woman."

"How's that?"

"There are four more *Alien* movies in your future. Maybe five."

That made Margo grin even more. Finn was certainly implying that these were movies that they would watch together, their future being of much more interest than that of the *Alien* franchise.

"I don't think Newhart appreciated the cat being in such danger," Margo added. "I don't know if he can handle five more *Alien* movies . . . but I can."

Finn let out a deep breath. Ten years of traveling, high-risk assignments, and solitary nights had led to a greater appreciation for this evening than Margo could even have guessed. But she could see his mind was churning.

"Franc for your thoughts?" she gently nudged.

He reached over to her sparkly pink quartz pendant and gently rested his knuckles against her collarbone. "This has got to be the prettiest thing I've ever laid eyes on."

"I bet you say that to all the necklaces."

And then the kiss that had been floating in the air as an idea became a warm, sweet reality. Margo felt his arms slide around her and pulled her in close. Such warm hands. And warm lips. And a warm chest. At that moment, witchly powers paled in comparison to this very common, but incomparable connection.

But regrettably, they had to pull themselves away from it as Finn was obligated to start a midnight shift at the police station.

"Yeah, gotta keep the town safe and patrol the beach, which I don't mind. Last time I did that, I ran into the most amazing girl." He pulled Margo in for one final kiss. "See you tomorrow. Now, you make sure that Newhart there sleeps it off."

Margo and Newhart both watched their favorite man make his exit. All in all, the evening had been a badly needed, euphoric respite. Both in her dreams and in her wakeful moments, Margo could feel Finn's warm knuckles resting against her chest. Murder, witchcraft, and uncertainty could wait.

CHAPTER TEN

I f she had put her mind to it, Fiona's Skretting could have become a very accomplished parallel parker. But it wasn't worth her bother. If two other cars were too difficult to squeeze between, then she had no intention of being inconvenienced.

So it was that Margo came across the striking sight of two driverless cars rolling gently away from one another until they bumped into adjoining vehicles. After which, Fiona's sporty black convertible slid into the now spacious parking spot.

Margo's walk slowed to a crawl. She had definitely spotted a witch, and one who was unconcerned about protecting her identity. Instinctively, Margo followed at a safe distance. A woman with a tiny poodle-mix dog crossed paths with Fiona. Her dog yipped and yapped at Fiona, and the owner smiled apologetically.

Fiona pointed a long, thin finger at the dog, whose mouth continued to open and close, but with no sound coming out. He had been muted like an annoying commercial. The owner stopped, confused and horrified. She gasped at Fiona, who arched an eyebrow and continued on her way.

Fiona's next victims were a family of five, including three extremely noisy, rambunctious children whose parents probably described them as exuberant. Fiona's patience for even well-behaved children was limited. For these irritating rugrats, it was nonexistent. One of them sprayed her with his water gun.

"I got her. I got her good."

"Oh, Lucas. Stop that. Sorry about that. But you should take that as a compliment. Because he only does that to goodhearted people who have a good sense of humor."

Boy, were they barking up the wrong tree. Fiona cocked her head for a moment, thinking of a suitable response. Then she regarded the family again as the hair of every one of them changed into a bright purple. As she walked away, she grinned evilly. "I have an excellent sense of humor."

The shriek of horror behind her only intensified her glee.

Margo's mouth dropped open. This witch was nothing like Delphine. This woman was downright scary. Margo dropped even farther back. She certainly didn't want Fiona to catch sight of her. But it was to no avail. Fiona was fully aware of her fascinated observer.

In fact, though she regularly engaged in mischief, she was laying it on particularly thick on this occasion, precisely because she knew Margo was watching. Word had spread that Lilith's organs had been distributed amongst the commoners. But clearly, none of these organ recipients could have more than a fraction of Lilith great powers, and Fiona was quite happy to remind the unworthy little fledgling witch who was now the top dog.

*****

Margo stood reverently in front of Lilith Hazelwood's tombstone. It was a beautiful polished gray granite, notably larger and more ornate than the vast majority of the surrounding headstones, just as Lilith would have insisted on, had she thought to make any funeral arrangements.

Margo wasn't sure why she hadn't come sooner. The only other occasions she'd ever come to the cemetery were to visit her mother. How different these two women were, and yet both had made her what she was. Her mother would always have her unwavering affection and devotion, even though Margo had never had a chance to know her. But her mother had given her a weak heart, and this witch had given her a strong one.

Delphine crept up behind Margo unnoticed. "I was surprised when you asked to meet here," Delphine said "Commoners usually find it a sad or frightening place. But most of us find it a very peaceful place, soulful, comforting. Are you already starting to feel that?"

"I'm trying to understand what it means to be a witch. I saw Fiona Skretting this morning. She was doing really mean things to people. She was terrifying. And she seemed to . . . get a kick out of it."

"I have always seen our powers as a gift. But without a doubt, they can be twisted into something else. There is nothing inherently evil about our community. And while I hesitate to characterize Fiona as an evil being, there is little about her that's good. Too much power can be conducive to excesses of recklessness, self-centeredness, maliciousness, and in the case of one who was only the second-most powerful witch in the community, bitterness. She bitterly resented Lilith Hazelwood, and I believe that bitterness consumed her and became her."

"But was Lilith like that?" Margo asked uneasily.

"Lilith? Imagine your favorite performer artist, musician, or actor. Someone whose talent fills you with awe and wonder. Suppose they were filled with ego and selfishness. They're a nightmare to work with, demanding, a diva. But their talent is sublime, so awe-inspiring that you make allowances for their extreme personality. You take the bad with the good. That was how I saw Lilith. She showed us the heights of our capabilities. It didn't matter that she couldn't be bothered to be a friend or mentor to any of us. I always hoped that she found some contentment in life as she chose to live it."

"You know, she's given me more than just a strong heart and the powers you've shown me."

"Her fearlessness."

"Yes! That part of her. But, I worry . . ."

"The essence of who you were before has not disappeared. You'll be enhanced by her strength, but you shouldn't fear being corrupted by her lesser tendencies."

Margo paused thoughtfully. "And Fiona Skretting. You say that she resented Lilith. You said that Lilith was killed. Fiona was also at the restaurant when Julian Meeks was killed. Delphine . . . did she do it? Any of it?"

"I wish I knew. She is a practitioner of the dark arts. There's no doubt of that. I think I understand why she would want to be rid of Lilith. But I cannot know why she would have targeted that particular commoner. I gather he was in a rather unpleasant business, but I don't think she had enough morality to be troubled by it. And he would have had to do something truly heinous to receive a death sentence. Even the dark arts are governed by laws of justice."

"With all of her powers, she probably knows something. She could probably tell me something useful or important about Julian Meeks's murder if she really wanted to," Margo speculated.

Delphine shook her head. "*If* she really wanted to, and I don't know why she would. And if she wasn't involved—and that is something that has not been ruled out—that is not a promising road to the answers you seek."

"But I'm running out of roads," Margo said grimly.

Delphine couldn't help but worry. The growing courage and stubbornness and determination in Margo were unlikely to be halted by an argument for caution. She could only hope that Margo presented so little threat to Fiona, that fact alone would help keep her safe.

*****

Lost in thought on her way back to work, Margo was stopped in her tracks by the mother of all déjà-vus. A group of bullies was shoving a younger boy, except this time, it was four to one. The cowardly advantage had Margo seething with anger, even from a great distance. She quickened her step and reached them in moments.

The victim's face was familiar, as were most of the bullies. They had come into the theater with their parents for some family classics, primarily in their younger years. The mothers would undoubtedly have cringed with shame to see their children behaving so brutally. From the smug, confrontational looks on their faces, that was unlikely to be a convincing argument. No matter. Margo was geared up for a fight.

"Can we help you?" the biggest one asked roughly.

"Yes. I was hoping to have a word with my old friend . . ." She snapped her finger, looking at the younger boy, trying to summon his name from memory.

"Lewis," the younger boy squeaked out.

"Lewis is indisposed," the leader of the group joked, leaving the others in fits of laughter.

"I think Lewis would prefer my company to hanging out with a bunch of spineless cowards whose idea of a fair fight is four to one."

"How about four on two?" the bully said menacingly.

"How about it?" Margo bristled, not backing down an inch. "Or can you only deal with someone smaller than you?"

"Bigger, smaller, nobody wins against us."

Margo got right in his face, her left hand grasping her pendant. "I suggest you go home."

"Carl, listen to *her*. She called you spineless, man. Want to show her your spine?"

Reminded of Margo's intolerable insults, the leader's face hardened. Almost in slow motion, Margo saw the punch coming. She saw the shoulder draw back and the fist clench. By the time it connected with her, she was ready.

"*Nesploro Fiere!*"

Carl's body jumped backward three feet and fell flat on the ground as if he had just touched an electrical fence. He started howling in pain. His buddies gathered around him. Their eyes, however, were still on Margo.

"Dude, what happened?"

"Get him up, get him up."

They dragged Carl to his feet. He was still shaken, but it was clear that the pain was over. He pointed at Margo.

"She's got some kind of taser. Yeah. Some kind of machine. I'm going to tell my parents. I'll tell the police too."

"I would love to have a sit down with your parents and talk to them about how you behave. I'm sure it will be a proud moment for them. What do you think? And the police? I've got a good friend on the police force. I think he, too, would dearly love to have a chat with you about ganging up on a smaller kid. I think we would all like to weigh in on that."

The boys soon came to the conclusion that the best course of action was to hightail it out of there.

"Why don't you walk with me?" Margo said to Lewis.

"How did you do that?" Lewis asked in awe.

"Did you ever see that movie, *Taken*? Well, Liam Neeson is not the only person with a particular set of skills."

"That was a really good movie," Lewis said, more impressed with Margo than Liam.

"Yeah? I only saw the previews. I never actually saw the movie. I thought it would be too scary for me."

The thought of anything being too scary for this bold, unflappable woman made Lewis shake his head.

Lilith nodded approvingly. Most of her afternoons trailing Margo were full of social pleasantries, dull business errands, and excruciating romantic nonsense. But this incident was one of the most promising that Lilith had witnessed to date. Margo's willingness to take action and use her powers, and inflict a little sting on an insufferable brat . . . all boded well for her future usefulness.

*****

Having secured Lewis's promise that he would give her a heads up if those boys so much as gave him a dirty look, Margo headed to *Margo's Movie House* to open up for the afternoon show. She still remembered the look of relief on his face, which certainly took away some of her misgivings about going all vigilante on the bully. She knew she hadn't inflicted any lasting damage, and she *knew* it because the amount of force had actually felt under her control. Besides, that punch would have hurt.

Margo couldn't help but think back to her conversation with Delphine just that morning. What kind of witch was she going to be?

Just before reaching the theater entrance, Margo glanced at the coffeehouse window next door and saw Dr. Svenson enjoying a frosty blended latte and perusing a medical journal. Dear Dr. Svenson. Nothing could diminish Margo's gratitude and high regard for him. However, she would've appreciated a fuller disclosure from him about how her life was about to be transformed.

"Margo. How nice to see you. I was hoping you might see me on your way to the theater. I know we have a checkup scheduled soon, but I always like to know that you're doing well."

"Oh, I'm doing very well. My heart lets me do all kinds of new and interesting things."

There were candles on the café table, a little atmosphere for the evening hours. Margo reached over and touched the wick on one of them.

"*Nesploro Fiere*," she whispered. The candle burst into flame. The doctor's face was, predictably, filled with amazement.

"What is this? Is this some kind of trick?" he marveled.

"No, Dr. Svenson. This is called being a witch," Margo said pointedly. "Why didn't you tell me that Lilith Hazelwood was a witch?"

This was not an unexpected confrontation. The doctor had known that he should eventually tell Margo the full story behind her heart. But it was something that she might have some mixed feelings about. He could assure her that Lilith's heart was just like any other human heart, just more robust, stronger, and younger. And beyond giving her an enviable endurance, it would not affect her life or capability in any other way. That's what he'd always planned on telling her. Now, she was telling him something quite different and it left him dumbfounded.

"This is impossible. You cannot become a witch. It is simply impossible."

Margo took his latte off the saucer it was perched on and pulled the saucer in front of her. "*Refractere.*" It quickly shattered.

The doctor swallowed hard, mind racing. What had he done? How could Margo Bailey be a witch? And at the same time, she was clearly blooming with health. That was certainly worth any . . . side effects, surely.

"What . . . were those words that you just said? How did you learn them?"

"Delphine Sykes is helping me to figure out how to use my powers. The powers that have come to me from Lilith Hazelwood's heart. And the anger. I used to be scared of getting angry. You told me never to let myself get worked up over anything. But Delphine shows me how to channel it into the magic. And then it's gone. Then it can't hurt me."

"No wonder. Perhaps she was trying to tell me this. She certainly must have known that day in the Hazlewood house."

"You really didn't know this would happen?"

"No. It's rather fascinating. It's extraordinarily fascinating. There are so many studies that need to be done."

Margo shook her head. "I don't want to be studied. I'm pretty sure that none of them want to be studied. They're just humans who want to be left alone and live their own lives. Yes, they can do some extraordinary things. They don't want to live in a laboratory, and neither would I. I hoped you might have some answers for me. But I'm going to have to find my own, and that's okay. I'm starting to become very glad that I have a witch's heart. I was so fragile before. Now I feel like I can do anything, face anything, not be scared of anyone."

"Margo, I'm glad you are feeling so strong. But do not forget how powerful Lilith Hazelwood was, and she still died. She was not immortal, and neither are you. I hope you will not behave recklessly. Just because you're no longer fragile does not mean that you can't break. I feel responsible for all of this."

Margo stood up. "You are responsible for saving my life." She bent over and gave him a kiss on the cheek. "See you later."

The doctor watched Margo walk to the theater with a bounce in her step. He still struggled to take in this unbelievable but undeniable reality. As little as he knew about Margo's new condition, he hoped she would take his advice. No recklessness. No unnecessary risk. It was perhaps just as well that Margo's actual plans were unknown to him.

*****

Margo was feeling emboldened the following afternoon. She'd had a lovely evening the previous night after work. Finn had stopped by and they had two hours to spend together before he had to leave for his police shift. They took a long walk on the moonlit beach, hand-in-hand, talking about families. Movies. Surfing.

Margo hadn't wanted to press him on the Meeks murder. She wouldn't want to violate his professional ethics. She looked forward to the day when the two of them could talk about everything. Everything! Including her new powers. Would he freak out? The doctor handled the news pretty well. But then, the doctor had knowingly put a witch's heart into her, so, yeah, he was a lot less surprised.

A few more intoxicating kisses before Finn headed off to work. He fussed a bit when she wouldn't accept a ride home. The moon was too big and glorious not to savor every moment of it. Maybe it was her imagination, but it felt positively energizing. Energy she would need the next day when she was determined that she would confront Fiona Skretting.

*****

Fiona lived quite a way inland. Her house was just yards away from a large, cool pine forest. Her house was a dark, somber gray, decidedly in contrast to homeowners who painted their colorful homes as if to keep the tourists in a good mood.

As Margo strode up the walkway with determination, the door opened, and there stood an ominously suspicious Fiona. She examined Margo from head to toe.

"Good. I was worried this was going to be a more memorable encounter."

"What . . . what do you mean?"

"I thought Lilith might have taken possession of your body and come to pay me a call."

Margo could not have been more taken aback. "She can *do* that?" she practically shouted at Fiona.

"I assume her spirit still retains some of its former strengths. Though I see you've inherited some portion. Well, come in. You've interrupted my coffee."

Margo breathed a sigh of relief. Coffee was normal, right? Maybe Fiona was more normal than she'd been led to believe. She followed her into the dark house. With closed curtains, Margo could hardly make out the outline of the furniture. She stumbled over a foot rest.

Fiona sighed, exasperated, and the living room lights all turned on at once. "My sight is keen without the light, but clearly, your talents are limited. Lilith could certainly do better for a host body, but then, I'm sure she's already figured that out for herself."

"Not a lot freaks me out these days, but this whole host body thing is a lot to wrap my head around."

Fiona was not a woman of patience. "Why are you here?"

"I was hoping you could help me."

"Do I look like a scout leader?"

"You look like the most powerful witch in Oyster Cove," Margo said, hoping to appeal to Fiona's ego. "I was sure you would have some special insight."

"Hmphh! Into what?"

"You were at Russell Knox's tapas restaurant the night that Julian Meeks was poisoned."

"Ah, yes. That was an exciting evening, wasn't it?"

"Or tragic, depending on how you look at things like that."

"I find the drama of commoners very entertaining."

"Even a murder?"

Fiona's grin was unapologetic. "What could be more entertaining? Hate. Pre-meditation. Anguish. And the extinction of life. I have an appreciation for high drama."

"I prefer old movies myself. Why were you there that night?"

Fiona tilted her head, determined to be as unhelpful as possible. "I'd heard wonderful things about his pot stickers. Well-deserved praise. Too bad Mr. Knox is headed for a life behind bars."

"He's innocent."

"Yes, he is. But that's a pretty hard thing to prove."

Margo was startled. "You know he didn't do it? Why were you really there that night?"

This was a cat and mouse game that Fiona couldn't resist. "There was a dark energy swirling over the roof that night. A destiny of death, moving toward fruition. It was not to be missed."

So there was no turning back. The question had to be asked. "Did you have anything to do with Julian Meeks's death?"

"What if I did? What if I had just cause to send him to the next world? What do you think you could do about it? And what makes you think you might not suffer the same fate?"

"I just want to get an innocent man out of jail."

"His suffering is of no consequence to me. I practice the dark arts as I see fit, and I answer to no one. You would be well advised to remember that. Has anyone suffered at my hands recently? That's a real possibility, isn't it? There's always someone about who deserves it. Now go. My coffee has gotten cold."

Just a light touch on the handle of her mug, and hot steam from the drink drifted into the air. Margo was so outmatched, it wasn't funny. And it wasn't safe. She fairly sprinted out of the house into the fresh air with a sigh of relief.

CHAPTER ELEVEN

S o that was the nightmare version of being a witch. If only Fiona's ethics were as strong as her powers. If Fiona Skretting was actually behind Julian Meeks's murder, how could it ever be uncovered or punished through the normal channels? It would never make it to the court system. Margo could only imagine how the police would respond to the accusation. Even Finn, exceptional fellow that he was, was likely to think she had lost her mind. Not that she was positive that Fiona was involved. She just had to acknowledge the depressing possibility that the real killer might never be found.

As luck would have it, the route from Fiona's house back to the center of town crossed the path of *Barcelona* restaurant. Sadly, it looked as if his fiancée had finally had to close it down. There was probably nothing of use to be found inside. But no harm in taking a final look.

Margo's intention was to use her abilities to break the lock. Someone had already beaten her to it. The lock had already been forced open. Vandals? She entered cautiously. The main eating area was dark and empty, but there was light in the hallway and in the kitchen beyond. She followed the lights all the way to Russell's office. There she found his brother, Walter, searching through the desk drawers.

"What are you doing here?" Margo demanded.

Walter jumped in fright. "Geez . . . you scared the bejeesus out of me. What are *you* doing here?"

"The door was open. Or should I say opened, and very forcefully. Which brings me back to, what are you doing here?"

"I'm Russell's brother. It's my responsibility to make sure that his affairs are in order."

"As Russell's brother, your responsibility actually was to make sure that your brother doesn't get put away for life for a crime that he didn't commit. But it's a little too soon to plan on the electric chair in any case. Why would you need to get his affairs in order?"

"You know . . . every business has bills to pay—utilities, landlord. I thought maybe I could take care of that for him."

"Wouldn't you need to have access to his business accounts?" Margo wondered skeptically.

"Well, I–I thought if I could find his bills and his business checkbook, then I could make sure his payments are current for him," Walter said haltingly.

"You're looking for his checkbook?" Margo asked pointedly.

"That's right. And may I ask again, what are you doing here?"

"Just returning to the scene of the crime."

"But you weren't here that night."

"But you were. You and Russell don't get along particularly well. What were you doing here the night that Meeks was poisoned?"

"I wanted to give Russell a piece of my mind. I was ticked off with him because he had been talking to all the relatives about . . ." Walter looked away awkwardly.

"About what?"

"Well, Russell was pretty keen on shutting off Grandpa's life support, which I had strenuous objections to, you know. It just seemed wrong."

"And when did it start seeming right? You have medical power of attorney and you've scheduled the life-support to be shut off."

Walter was genuinely surprised that Margo knew so much about his plans. "Did Russell tell you that? I didn't even think that he knew it was scheduled. Well, he'd better not have any complaints. It's exactly what he has been saying all along. It was his idea, all this time. I just finally . . . have come to see the sense in it. Grandpa's either unconscious or he's suffering. That's no way to live. It's the right thing to do."

"You didn't think so two weeks ago," Margo countered.

"I still don't know what you doing here."

"Trying to see if there's anything I can do for Russell."

"Well, tell him to say a little prayer for Grandpa tomorrow morning. 'Cause he sure won't be able to be present at the . . . ceremony."

Tomorrow morning! This was terrible. Russell might still be found innocent in court if the case could be made for reasonable doubt. But he would still have lost his inheritance. And his restaurant, possibly, by having it burned to the ground. If not that, he wouldn't have the money to rebuild his lost customer base due to the scandal. Tomorrow would be the end of his dreams, his hopes, his hard work. Unless there were some way of stopping it.

First, she wasn't going to let Walter help himself to Russell's blank checks. "As soon as I step outside, I'm going to call the police and tell them that the restaurant has been broken into by vandals. I suggest you make yourself scarce."

Walter's jaw dropped. Margo was a lot more formidable than she first appeared.

*****

The woman at the hospital desk shook her head at Margo sympathetically. "You are a friend of the family?"

"Yes, and Walter said it would be all right if I joined them tomorrow for Mr. Knox's final goodbyes. But I just wanted to double-check on the time. I sort of remembered five p.m. Can you look that up for me?"

"Sure, let me just pull that up." The woman went through the motions of getting the information about her computer screen. "It's nine a.m."

"Oh, no. That sounds way too early. I'm sure I would've remembered it was in the morning. What if the family comes too late? Could you check on the original permission slip that Walter signed just so that there's no misunderstanding?"

"Yeah, I can get those."

She stood up and unlocked a tall file cabinet behind her. "Knox. Here it is. Hmm. Yes. Nine a.m. We put the right time in the computer."

"Isn't that something. Could I see that please?"

"Sure, here you go."

The woman returned to her seat and took a phone call. Margo smiled gratefully, turned her back to the woman, and swiftly reduced the original document into a smoldering ash. She laid the manila folder back on the counter, and the woman nodded distractedly as Margo dashed away. She knew that new papers could be filled out, but Walter had mentioned a mandatory ten-day grace period. Just a little reprieve. If only she could make the most of it.

*****

Thus far, Margo had pilfered documents out of Ian Fowler's business cabinet, destroyed hospital records, and gone medieval on a teenaged brat. While each of these could be justified—hey, the last one was for self-defense—she still couldn't help but worry that she was skirting a little too close to the dark side. That was definitely not the kind of witch she wanted to be.

"Teach me something nice," Margo demanded of Delphine. "Not destroying, breaking, or zapping. Teach me something that will make people happy. I don't want to be a bad witch. I want to know how to do nice things. Teach me something nice."

"I don't doubt your goodness, Margo, and you shouldn't either. There is a "good" way of using everything that you've been taught. However, there are a few fun things. . . *Severnay.*"

The lights and electricity went out.

"That should be an easy one for you with your special talent with electricity. *Seterno.*"

And the lights popped back on.

"Very handy for when you're coming home after dark or are carrying an armful of groceries."

"Or when you're in bed and remember that you forgot to turn the basement light off," Margo mused. "*Severnay.*"

The lights went off again.

"You're a natural. Electricity was completely under Lilith's command."

"*Seterno.*" And it worked like a charm—lights back on. "I'm a human Clapper."

"You could probably shut down all the lights of a very large building. Not that there's much call for that. Oh. I have another one for you."

There was a vase full of pink flowers on the coffee table in front of them. It was Bette's doing. She thought it added a cosmopolitan touch to the room. Delphine touched the edge of one of the pink petals.

"*Resplenda.*"

The flower turned sky-blue, and one by one, the other flowers in the bouquet followed suit. Margo squealed. That's exactly what she had in mind.

"Or perhaps yellow would match your walls better," Delphine mused. She touched the petals again, and the bouquet became bright lemon yellow. She was gratified to see Margo's appreciation. She stood up and walked over to the wall. "On second thought, I don't think that yellow matches your walls at all. We may have to change the color." She touched the wall, and its soft moss green was quickly transformed to a deep burgundy. Margo was dazzled. It was like being in a whole new house.

"Yes, please. That's what I want to know how to do. But you said the same word each time, even though it made different colors happen. How did you do that?"

"You only have to keep the desired color in your mind. Imagine it. Love the color. And it will pour out of you."

As Delphine watched Margo's delight with the new lesson, she was reminded that she and all the other witches had been taught their first magic lessons when they were children. Changing the colors of objects was much like commoner children being absorbed in their coloring books. Animating their little dolls and having them prance around the room were all part of a little witch's development. In other words, there was no harm in backtracking a bit and teaching Margo some youthful thrills.

*****

Delphine had left for the day, and Margo was gathering her beach things together. She had a special afternoon surprise for Finn. As she went to gather up Newhart into his carrier, the cat let out a yell and hightailed it up the stairs. That was unfortunate. She was sure he was becoming a lot more secure and less skittish, especially about the whole feet issue. But now, he had just taken off as if he'd seen a . . .a ghost. And Margo quickly realized that he probably had. It wasn't the first time that she wondered about Lilith's presence or had sensed herself being watched.

Her benefactor. The woman whose death had made her life possible. Margo sank slowly back onto the sofa and tried to think of the right words.

"Lilith Hazelwood. I know you're there. I wish I could you see was well as my cat does. I know that Delphine can see you and speak to you. I just wanted you to know . . . I know that something terrible happened to you. At least, Delphine tells me that your death was not an accident. And as much as I wanted to live, I never wanted that to happen to anyone.

I hope you understand how much your heart means to me. Not just because it has made me healthy and strong and has given me a future. But it was filled with your courage, your fearlessness, your certainty. I've lost so much of my fear of life, and for that, I'll be forever grateful.

I know that we are two very different people. Very different. And maybe if we had come face-to-face in life, you would have despised my weakness. I probably would have been terrified of you. It's only in sharing the same heart that we have become connected. I hope that I can live in such a way that shows just how grateful I am for this incredible gift. *But don't take over my body. Please don't take over my body.*

I have to go now. When you have a great heart, it really pushes you to try to do something great every day. So thank you again, Ms. Hazelwood. I did ask Delphine to tell you as much, but I wanted to tell you myself."

Lilith watched the girl exit her home, not knowing what to make of this naïve creature. She was haunting this girl, stalking her, and yet the girl behaved as if she had a guardian angel. Well, the gratitude was appropriate enough. And it could be exploited under the right circumstances.

*****

Finn had heard about the popular cliff diving spot some ten miles outside Oyster Cove. He hadn't taken a lot of interest in it, though. Tall heights left him more than a bit queasy. He wasn't sure of the origin of that particular phobia. Had he taken a spill at an early age that was now beyond the recall of memory? Or was it just a quirk of birth, hardwired into his brain's idiosyncrasies?

But Margo had suggested meeting at the spot to watch the daredevils do their thing, which would be entertaining enough. Apparently, the dive spot was so deep that no one had ever hit the bottom, and no accidents had ever been reported. Good thing, as this was not a designated public beach and there was no lifeguard posted.

Finn was the first to arrive. He chose a sitting spot with a good view of the ledge. Geez, moving by the sea was a great idea. Fresh ocean air. Pretty, lively tourist spot. Great seafood. And Margo. That was the one bonus that surpassed all the others. So many years on the road, so many nights in hotels and motels, so many fleeting relationships that couldn't be pursued because his work was dangerous and kept him on the go. All the while, he'd fantasized about this dream that couldn't possibly exist. And then one night, there she was, doing a clumsy cartwheel under a beautiful full moon. How did he get to be so lucky?

Finn's attention was drawn back to the divers hundreds of feet above, on the cliff. That's funny. That red and white bikini and that long, curly hair made that diver look a lot like Margo. Why—why was she waving at him? Margo!

He felt his stomach fly all the way up to his throat as he saw Margo step off the cliff, arms raised in victory. After she plunged into the water, Finn leapt to his feet in a panic. He needed to get out to her. He needed to know that she was fine. But . . . what was that? Another dolphin? He watched a tall fin swim to Margo's entry spot and disappear underwater. Was it a dolphin? Finn grabbed his gun. What if it was a shark? Would his gun work underwater? No time to think. He plunged into the water, clothes, gun, and all.

Margo was enjoying the view underneath the waves—the schools of fish, the dancing algae below, and the sun's weak refracted beam. Oh, and what was this? Like Finn, her first thought was dolphin. The shark showed his vicious teeth from fifteen yards away as it was closing in on her. Did he think that he was going to put an end to her?

Since acquiring her new heart, Margo's default response was not fear, but anger. As luck would have it, she was in the habit of never removing her pendant. "*Nesploro Fiere!*" The words were blurred by water but strengthened by her fury. The shark drew back in pain and confusion. Its dinner had just turned into a formidable adversary. Still stinging, it darted back out to sea. Margo let herself drift to the surface, where she saw Finn plowing toward her at full steam.

"Margo! Margo!"

She felt him wrap his body around her, a nice, warm shield against the cold water.

"Finn, you've got your clothes on."

"Yeah. I thought . . . I thought . . . was that a shark?"

Margo hesitated. "I don't think there have been any shark sightings around here. There are lots of other things that have big fins."

"Oh, yeah? I guess this city boy only knows about sharks."

"We should go in. Did you like my dive?"

"You're going to give me gray hair and a heart attack."

Back on shore, they shivered gladly in each other's arms. Margo had proven to herself once again that her new heart made all things possible. Meanwhile, Finn was left wondering what kinds of tricks his mind was playing on him. Margo was safe and nothing else really mattered, but what on earth had just happened?

"That's a 200-foot jump," Finn said incredulously.

"I highly recommend it. Seriously, you should give it a try."

"Oh, no. Bad guys and bullets, I can handle. Heights? Now don't laugh. I'm not good with heights. But you are just blowing my mind. Never swam in the ocean until two weeks ago, or were you just pulling my leg?"

She couldn't come clean about everything, but it seemed important that he should know something about what her life had been like. "Finn, I used to be scared of everything, the ocean most all—undertows, rip tides, jellyfish, eels, drowning, hurricanes, tsunamis . . ."

"New England tsunamis?"

"You should know that something doesn't have to actually exist for someone to be afraid of it. That's right, tsunamis. I've seen them on the news."

"So how is it, now, that you're not scared of anything? Did all the fears just gradually go away?

"They did go away, although there was nothing gradual about it. I guess it's just important to me right now to push myself to do things, to face things that used to scare me."

Finn was equal parts admiration and alarm. She was extraordinary, no two ways about it. But he was well-acquainted with the dangers of the world. Someone facing down her fears could put herself in a very precarious spot.

*****

Regretfully, Finn had to leave Margo to catch a few winks after his overnight shift. They would meet up again after the last theater show. Bette had loaned Margo her car for the day, as the cliff diving spot was so far outside Oyster Cove. Before she dropped the car off at Bette's hotel, Margo thought it would be nice to drop in on Delphine. Beyond her value as a magic tutor, Margo was really starting to enjoy her company.

But as she drove down the boardwalk, she saw a familiar face and a commotion that compelled her to pull over. Walter Knox's snazzy red Lexus was being towed, and Walter was in a loud screaming match with the repo man.

"I told you guys that I would have your money by the end of this week. And . . . things got a little messed up. So it will be, you know, maybe a week and a half later. But it's guaranteed. I'm getting an inheritance. I just have to have my grandpa die, but it's a done deal because we're removing the life-support ASAP so you fellas can get your money."

"That is the sickest thing I've ever heard," the repo man said with a disgusted look. "Now you get out of my face, or I will smack you down in the memory of my sainted grandmother who recently left this world. Respect your elders. That's what I always say. Respect your elders."

With a warning finger in Walter's face, the repo man turned to get into his truck and drove away with Walter's car. Margo came up from behind him.

"Need a ride?" she asked innocently.

Walter whirled around. "What? A ride from you? Why would you give me a ride? You just tried to call the police on me the other day."

"Believe it or not, Russell's very sad about losing his grandpa. He's going to miss him and would like to have a photo of him. You've got to have some family photos around that I could take to Russell." *Lilith must've been a pathological liar. This was all coming so easily.*

"Why would I do that for him? Or for you?"

"Because otherwise, you have a long walk ahead of you. A generous, charitable act is a reasonable exchange for a fifteen-minute drive, don't you think? Up to you."

"All right. All right. I live up by the golf course."

"Get in."

Walter was fuming for the majority of the ride. "If the hospital hadn't lost those records, that check would be on its way to me. I'd have my car. All those bill collectors would be off my back."

Margo remembered that Walter was her friend, Clarissa's, accountant. He probably had a ton of clients in Oyster Cove. Why was he so broke? And then she remembered Russell saying that their grandfather had been reluctant to leave his money to such a reckless gambler. That might explain why he wasn't paying his bills. And why he was rifling through Russell's office looking for blank checks. This guy was a piece of work.

So was his house, actually. It was a modern architectural showstopper and looked to be about 4000 square feet. It wasn't exactly Margo's style, but it was undeniably impressive. It also had Margo thinking that the mortgage was probably so high that a housing repo couldn't be far behind. As they walked to the front door, Walter regarded Newhart's case distastefully. "I don't know about that."

"It's too hot to leave him in my car. That's really dangerous."

Walter grunted reluctantly. Inside, Margo could see that Walter and his wife had sprung for deluxe professional decoration. It was as impeccably styled as a hotel suite. Clearly, Walter aspired to a grand lifestyle, but his gambling losses threatened to sink the whole ship. Just how desperate might he have gotten?

Margo wasn't the only one learning new tricks. Newhart had learned to bat at his latch at just the right angle to undo it. He sprang from his cage triumphantly and jetted off to the next room.

"Unbelievable!" Walter yelled.

"I'll get him," Margo said.

"He's gonna get fur all over the place."

"Sorry." Margo took off after her cat. He didn't go far, just into the dining room. He leaped to the top of the large dining room table, which was strewn with overdue bills and collection threats. What kind of an accountant was this? Margo had to wonder—surely, her friend Clarissa would never entrust him with her finances if she saw how careless he was with his own money.

"You and your cat need to get out of here. This is private stuff. This is not your business."

"No, it's not my business. And I'm sorry to have seen it. But I have seen it. You just put a $20,000 payment on this card. I'm sorry my cat walked past that. I couldn't help but see it. And you still owe another $20,000 on that card. But what I'd like to know is, where'd you get $20,000 for a payment? My friend Clarissa from *The Clam Shack* is one of your clients. Is her money safe? Is all of your clients' money safe?"

Walter bristled. "What are you trying to imply?"

"If there were an audit on Clarissa's business account, would every dime be accounted for?"

"'Course it would. I just . . . you know, I just need a little heads up. That's the way it works sometimes. Shift the money from here to there. It's called juggling."

"It's called embezzlement."

"Just hold it right there. I'm going to replace every dime that I borrowed from anyone's account. My grandfather's inheritance is over one million dollars. Everyone gets a clean book. All the bill collectors go away. And I get to start all over with a clean slate."

"But what would you have done if the murder had never happened? It was a pretty freakish event, right? Something you could never have counted on. What were you going to do to make everything right?"

Walter felt like yelling, but he could see that the best course of action was to try to win Margo's trust. She could get him in a whole lot of trouble.

"I would have been up the creek. That's about the size of it. But Russell got involved in this murder. Nothing to do with me. And now the inheritance is headed my way. You've gotta play the cards you're dealt. And every once in a while, you get a straight flush."

"Spoken like a true gambler," Margo noted.

"So, I don't need you stirring up trouble. Causing any panic. Soon, I'll have more than enough money to go around."

Not if I can help it, Margo thought. "I've got to get to work."

"Yeah, yeah. Let me get that picture for you."

Margo dutifully waited for the photo, holding down Newhart's cage, who wanted to try his new trick again.

"Here you go," Walter said, handing her a sweet old photo. "So are we cool?"

"You make sure you square up with everyone, and sure, we're cool." Margo didn't think it was a good idea to raise alarm in a man who was still on her list of murder suspects. She was spending an awful lot of time in the company of murder suspects.

CHAPTER TWELVE

The end of every night at the theater had now become Margo's favorite time of day. Finn was in the habit of stopping by for a few hours before his midnight shift began. Except tonight, he had a day off, and they wouldn't have to cut their evening short, which was nice. Sometimes, at her urging, he would even catch the evening show and she would slip in and sit beside him. After all, his film education had numerous holes in it. She was horrified to find out he had never even heard of *12 ANGRY MEN*.

"That was stellar," Finn said, genuinely impressed. "You really know how to pick 'em."

"It always inspires me. You know. Justice. The truth destined to come out. People overcoming their preconceptions. I must've watched it at least three or four times now. You know what we should do? You talked about night surfing and how much fun that was. That's what we should do. Why don't we try night surfing tonight?"

"Oh, I dunno. I think you've had enough excitement for one day."

"I have?"

"Yeah. That cliff diving and . . . everything. Why not just relax, take it easy. Let's go next door and grab a bowl of clam chowder."

"Okay. I like clam chowder. But I think I would like night surfing too. Oh, let me just get these trash bags first," Margo remembered.

"No, I got them. You just sit here and I'll just be a minute."

"Well, there are three bags. So you could do two and I'll do one."

"No, you just rest. Let me make myself useful."

Rest? Hadn't Margo just been sitting through a movie for almost two hours?

Soon enough, they were inside *The Clam Shack* and downing bowls of creamy chowder.

"You know what we could do after this? We can watch a scary movie. I know you have to have a lot more DVDs. How about that *Alien* sequel?" Margo suggested.

"Or, something a little more . . . laid back. One of your old classics, maybe."

Margo examined Finn intently as he tried to look away innocently.

"Who told you?"

"Told me what?"

"About my heart transplant."

Finn sighed. "I bumped into your sister on my way home this afternoon. And I mentioned the cliff diving. And she thought you were out of your mind. And she thought it was a good idea for me to know about the heart transplant. She's absolutely right. Margo, why didn't you ever tell me?"

"Because everyone has always treated me kindly and gently and with kid gloves. It was great to be treated as normal. No pity, no kid gloves, but as if I were strong, capable."

"You are beyond capable. But for an operation so recent, it seems a risky thing. You just got this new heart."

"But it passes every test I throw at it. It never lets me down. Do you know what the first twenty-five years of my life were like? Can you imagine wondering every day whether you're going to be alive tomorrow?"

"Hmm. Now you mention it, I suppose I do. A lot of my colleagues and friends never made it home from their last assignments. Smart, brave guys. No mistakes. Just bad luck. And sometimes, a little too much courage. So, I did have to prepare myself mentally for a short life, for life ending in the line of service. It was the last thought going through my head every night."

"Yes, and the first thing you would think about every morning—is this my last morning?" Margo said.

"Is this my last meal?" Finn added. "This roast is dry—this had better not be my last meal."

They chuckled together.

"Did you write a will?" Margo asked.

"Oh, I've had one for six or seven years now. Not that I have that much to pass on. The car. Chunk of savings. Most of my savings is going to Zoe."

"I wrote my first will when I was eight. Just as soon as I learned that my mother and I had the same heart condition. Everything I owned, down to my Chinese checkers set, had to be formally accounted for in my bequests. I've done that for almost twenty years. And you know what? I don't want to think about leaving life anymore. I'd rather think about living it. You know, really living. It feels like I have so much time to make up for. I can't play it safe anymore. Worrying about the worst things that can happen. Being careful and cautious about everything. I'm strong now. I don't want you to think of me as weak. Ever. I'm not."

Finn reached for her hand. "I won't. So, whatever you want to do tonight is fine by me. You name it, we'll do it."

Margo gripped his hand. "I want you to take me home, get into my bed, and make my heart *pound.*"

Finn's mouth hung open for a few split seconds before his thundering voice caused all nearby diners to turn around. "Check!"

Margo grinned. Hallelujah.

*****

Margo's heart held up just fine.

Around ten o'clock in the morning, they heard Bette come in and rummage around the kitchen. They didn't mind waiting her out, enjoying the dreamlike novelty of a morning wrapped around each other.

When Margo felt certain her sister had probably fallen asleep, they tiptoed out and down the stairs and headed quietly to the kitchen. There on the counter, they found a bowl of batter, the sign next to it saying, "Make him pancakes."

*****

Since Margo did have a picture of Russell's grandfather in her possession, it only seemed right pass it on. Finn gave her a ride to the station, and then they had tentatively planned on catching a mid-afternoon surfing session. From the station lobby, they could hear a big, angry commotion coming from the visitor's room.

"Who's got visitors?" Finn asked.

"Russell Knox. These guys say they had something financial to work out with him. But I think we have ourselves a situation."

Finn rushed down the hallway, and Margo was on his heels. In the visiting room, Julian Meeks's brother, Carson Meeks, was straining to get his hands on Russell and was being held back by Julian's cousin, Lester Quinn.

"You messed with the wrong family," Carson shouted. "That was my brother. That was my blood. Your days are numbered, buddy. My brother's gotta die because you owe him fifty grand? That's how you get out of paying your debts? You make me sick. Lethal injection is too good for ya. You made him suffer. No way should you get the easy way out."

Finn pulled Carson back and handed him to two officers behind him. "Mike, Barney, get him outta here."

"Just calm down, okay? Just calm down," Barney told Carson sternly.

The two officers led Carson Meeks out of the room.

"What was that about?" Finn asked.

"This guy owed our family fifty grand, like my cousin said. He signed a deal with Julian, and it was really starting to look like he wasn't going to hold up his end of the bargain. Jules was a tough guy, maybe a little harsh with him. But that's what you gotta do when you lend money. Carson's a hothead. But I get where he's coming from. We're all pretty upset about Julian. We need to see some justice. Now, I gotta get out here and get to my lumber office."

Margo drew closer to Russell. "Are you okay?"

"They're never going to believe me."

"Does Julian's family know about the arson threats and the fire insurance?"

"If they do, it just gives them more reason to think that I killed their brother."

"What's this? Arson? Fire insurance?" Finn inquired warily.

Margo thought it best to step outside the police station to explain to Finn the rather damaging motive that might lead a lot of people to believe that he was a killer. As she supplied one detail after another, Margo watched as Finn got madder and madder.

"How long have you known this?"

"A little while. A couple of weeks. The thing is, his lawyer told him not to tell the police. Because it would just be used against him. Because it looks like a really serious motive. And no one would even think about investigating other suspects if they believed Russell had such a strong reason to kill Julian Meeks."

"Yeah, that's exactly what it looks like. That was the missing piece—the motive I didn't quite have a handle on. It was too random, too unconnected. They knew each other, which he lied about. Julian Meeks was about to ruin him. Reason enough to kill. I can't believe you knew all this, Margo. You knew, and you never said a word."

"I don't believe that Russell did this. I really don't. And I don't want to get him in trouble. He finally got to this good point in his life, and now it's all been taken away. He doesn't deserve this. He really needs someone on his side now."

"I thought you said you barely knew him. That's right, isn't it? That visiting him here was pretty much the first time you spoke to him in your life. Which still doesn't explain to me why you took such an interest in someone you barely knew. What's up with that?"

"We . . . grew up in the same town," Margo said feebly. "We went to the same school at the same time."

"You're keeping things from me. Which doesn't work for me. Not as a cop. And not as someone who I thought was getting close to you. I thought we had some real trust here. But maybe we don't. In either direction."

He turned away and walked back into the station. Margo turned away woodenly and wandered off in a daze. What had she done?

*****

Finn was right. Why, why, why hadn't she confided in him? Margo just hadn't wanted to help put the final nail in Russell's coffin. It would have been too easy for Finn and the police force to completely give up on following any other leads. But now he was mad at her, and after their wonderful night together. What if his feelings about her had changed? She had to figure out some way to make this right.

It would help if she had someone to talk to. Bette? That would actually feel a bit hypocritical. Margo didn't know when she would ever be able to let her sister know about her newfound powers. But how could she talk about keeping secrets from Finn when she was also keeping such a big one from Bette?

Delphine. That's who she needed to talk to. In the short time they'd known each other, she had become so comfortable with the older woman. So safe. It was nice to have someone who she could say anything to . . . someone she didn't have to hide anything from.

Margo rounded the corner to the street Delphine's boutique was on, and for the second time in as many days, she was met with the sight of Walter Knox. This time was quite a bit more surreal than seeing him have his car repo-ed. He was standing right next to Delphine, their bodies angled away from Margo.

Walter's hand was outstretched and Delphine was counting cash bills into it. Crisp bills that even from a distance looked a lot like hundred-dollar bills. What on earth could Delphine be paying Walter for? Margo didn't even know the two them knew one another.

But what she did know was that she had rattled on enough about Julian Meeks's murder, and her own attempts to uncover the truth, and that she had most certainly mentioned Walter's name to Delphine. If she knew him, why wouldn't she have said so? And again, why was she giving him money?

They were in front of Delphine's business. Any normal transaction should have had money going in her direction, not his. But then, he was an accountant—perhaps Delphine was one of his clients. But no one pays their accountant in cash. Check usually. PayPal, possibly. Something business appropriate.

All of a sudden, Margo was on the very uncomfortable end of having a secret kept from her by a trusted friend. The payout continued till it amounted to what Margo would have estimated as $2000. What service had Walter performed for Delphine to get such a nice compensation?

Margo drew back into a doorway to remain unseen. Delphine returned to her shop and Walter took off briskly down the road. Margo scurried after him. There was no reason to think that a direct confrontation would be fruitful. But she did want to know what he was up to.

It was entirely predictable that Walter was headed directly to his car dealership. He was going to get his car back, apparently, courtesy of Delphine. Which brought Margo's thinking back to Delphine—who was someone Margo had taken at her word, never questioned, and knew very little about.

*****

It was much earlier than she needed to get to the theater, but sometimes, the lobby sitting area served as a cozy little oasis of solitude. A place to think things through. As Margo approached her theater, she could see a man reading the posters and reviews right outside. But his back was to her, and she didn't see that it was restaurant owner Ian Fowler until she was right on him.

"Well, look who we have here. A little thief. You have a lot of nerve going into my things. Taking things that don't belong to you."

"I was taking things that didn't belong to *you*. You messed Russell Knox up, but good. Delayed his restaurant's opening. Got him in trouble with his creditors. You want to take me to court? That would necessitate your explaining how those documents came into your possession. I believe the operative concept here is mail fraud, with malicious intent."

"You got me in hot water with the cops. They not only wanted to talk to me about those letters, but about poisoning the dead guy and things that have absolutely nothing to do with me. He wanted to look over the office and the kitchen, but I said no warrant, no search. Look at the mess you got me in."

"You're a free man, which is more than Russell Knox can say."

"You can get yourself into some serious trouble if you keep messing with me." There was a menacing tone behind the implied threat.

"Don't you have a dinner shift to get ready for?" Margo was not in a mood to be intimidated.

"You think about what I just said."

"What I'm thinking is that I would love a plate of yummy tapas. And I'll bet hundreds of folks in Oyster Cove would agree." She arched an eyebrow at him, slipped into the theater, and left him fuming. Two months ago, that man would have had her cowering, assuming she would ever have had the nerve to do anything to cross him, which she hadn't. *Thank you, Lilith.*

*****

Finn mindlessly pushed the eggs over easy around on his plate. He was at his favorite diner, one he stopped by often on his way home after the all-night shift. The last sixteen hours had been a torturous anxiety. He had been awfully rough on Margo. Perhaps he should have given her the benefit of the doubt. He paid for the barely eaten meal and stumbled out into the street— where he found Margo standing, waiting for him. The relief of seeing her was almost enough to make him forget how mad he was supposed to be. Almost.

"Russell was a year behind me in junior high, so I never paid him any attention. I never even knew his name," Margo began. And so she gave the full detailed account of that bullying event that had left her with such shame and regret.

She was well aware that it was likely to sound silly or pathetic or a lie. The event was obviously more traumatic for Russell Knox than for herself, and yet he had been able to move past it with flying colors, creating a great life for himself prior to the recent unfortunate turn of events. It hadn't held him back. It hadn't even caused him to hold any resentment toward her. So it was hard to convey why it had affected her so, why it had burdened her soul and why she felt that she owed it to Russell to help him out now in his time of need. Not for the sake of an old friendship that had never existed, but for decency. For atonement.

"That was one of the worst things about my old heart. Knowing that I couldn't ever help anyone. Feeling so useless. I still don't know if I can help Russell now. But I have to try. I owe him that. And I should've told you that. Not because you're a cop, but because you're my . . . my—"

Finn came close to her and dropped his forehead down till it lightly touched hers.

Margo sighed. "I wasn't sure if you'd understand."

"Understand that my supercool girlfriend just keeps getting cooler and cooler?"

Margo leaned into him with an audible sigh of relief. "So, we're good, then?"

"Absolutely. In fact, we should shake on it. Full body shake. Over at your place."

"Oh, I see. You were very highly motivated to forgive me. Lucky for you, we're on the same page, but Bette is probably going to be home soon."

"Oh . . . maybe she'll make us pancakes."

"No shame."

Finn threw an arm around her shoulder and steered her toward his car. He stopped for a moment to answer his cellphone. Margo had a hard time reading the strange look on his face. He hung up.

"Guess who just made bail?"

Margo had no problem guessing. But how? Russell's bail had been set for $100,000.

"Who could have done that? That's a lot of money," Margo marveled.

"Family?"

"His family doesn't have any money. Neither does his fiancée."

"Well, I hate to delay the . . . pancakes. But, we need to see what's going on."

Margo nodded gratefully. She wasn't sure how it was coming about, but Russell seemed one step closer to freedom.

*****

Russell was retrieving the small stash of possessions he had brought with him to the jail. He greeted Margo's entry with a look of stunned gratitude.

"I was wondering if this was your doing," he said to her.

"I do not sell enough popcorn and Raisinets to ever have a spare hundred grand lying around. No. It wasn't me."

"Nobody gave you a heads up?" Finn asked Russell. "Any special visitors in the last few days?"

"No. I mean, a lot of people have expressed their support. There were even a couple of editorials in the paper saying they didn't think I did it. But I don't know anyone who could help me like this."

"Yeah, we saw those editorials. *Free Russell.* Maybe there was some effort to raise money?" Finn wondered.

"A Kickstarter?" Margo offered. "We should have thought of that. Where's your fiancée?"

"I called her. She had to get a temp job after the restaurant closed. She really wanted to be here, but the job pays well, and we're going to need that money, whatever happens. But especially if I wind up going back in."

"Need a ride somewhere?" Finn asked.

"No reason to rush home—Wendy's not there. It's been so long since I could walk around and since I had a meal that wasn't capped off with green Jell-O. I think I'm just going to stretch my legs. Thanks, though."

"Well, my boss wants to go over the particulars of this case. Why don't you walk your buddy out?" Finn suggested to Margo. "I'll give you a call in an hour."

"Sure." Her plans with Finn could wait another hour. Russell really looked as if he could use the company.

As they stepped outside, Russell shielded his eyes against the bright sunlight. "The little outdoor space they let me wander around in was shaded. Which was for my benefit, I guess. But it's been too long since I've felt the sun beating on me."

"I can imagine. Or I probably can't. What would you like to do? Anywhere. Anything."

"Oh, definitely the beach. Fried clams. And a gelato."

They laughed.

"Green Jell-O, huh? Yeah, we can do better than that."

Margo and Russell stepped into the street, the street lights and spotlights having given them the right of way. There was a car approaching that had slowed down appropriately as they stood on the curb. But as they stepped into the street, it sped up and headed straight toward them. Margo spotted it first, grabbing Russell's arm and yanking him back behind the tall streetlight pole. The car veered away, squealing out of control, and skidded into a parked car on the opposite side with a hard crash.

CHAPTER THIRTEEN

They had not gotten a great distance from the police station. Soon, they were surrounded by cops and ambulances.

"You okay?"

"Yeah, we're okay. Who . . . who was that?"

It was the brother of poison victim Julian Meeks, Carson Meeks. He was going to have to be taken to the hospital with a number of minor injuries and then transferred to the jail. But he was still conscious and fuming angrily.

"That devil killed my brother. My family is going to get justice. You'd better know it. I won't rest until that guy is in his grave. I was willing to spend a hundred grand to get this guy close enough to get his just desserts. And it ain't over. It'll never be over till he's paid for taking my brother away."

Yes, that was Russell's secret benefactor, so enraged that he had gladly paid the $100,000 bail to remove the safety of Russell's prison bars and make him available for final justice.

Finn, Margo, and Russell retreated back to the police station.

"Who's got that kind of money to throw around?" one cop marveled. "That is a lot of hate right there. You sure you wouldn't rather stay here, where you're nice and safe?' he taunted Russell.

"I would not." Russell bristled. "I've been waiting too long to get out of here."

"Hold your horses," Finn warned. "Carson Meeks is in custody. But is he the only nutcase in the family? We don't know. I need to have a word with my boss."

Margo and Russell watched Finn confer with his captain. Meanwhile, Lester Quinn came storming in with his very pregnant wife, Rowena, close behind.

"I was just at the hospital. They won't let me talk to my cousin. What's up with that?"

"Your cousin just tried to kill two people," Finn answered angrily.

"I think I was just incidental," Margo added. "He wanted to kill Russell."

Lester was confused. "What's this guy doing out of jail, anyway?"

"Maybe you should check his bank account. There'll be a hundred grand missing that he used to pay bail to get Mr. Knox out on the streets so he could take a shot at him. Your cousin is going to be in prison for a very long time," Finn said, seething. Carson's relatives were not to blame for what had just happened, but Finn had come way too close to losing Margo and he was not in a sympathetic mood.

"Oh, no," wailed Rowena. "My water! My water just broke."

The police chief sighed. "Get the ambulance over here."

"No, I'll drive her. It's faster," Lester insisted.

"All right. We can give them an escort," the chief said.

"I'll do it," Barney volunteered. "No problem."

There was a flurry of action as Rowena was escorted out.

"And Cochran," the chief said to Finn, "We'll cover the safe house until we get this sorted out."

"All right," Finn said to Margo and Russell. "Let's go."

*****

"Where are we?" Margo asked as Finn drove up to a nondescript motel a few miles outside town.

"The police department is going to cover the tab for a safe house. We booked two rooms. Neither of you should be at your homes. Not until we know there aren't going to be any more vendettas coming your way."

"Well, okay, that's probably a good idea for him," Margo said. "But no one's trying to kill me. I was just standing next to . . . the wrong person. No offense."

"You just saved the wrong person's life. So, none taken," Russell said gratefully. "But, I have got to see Wendy and let her know what's going on."

"Leave that to me. I'll tell her you're safe," Finn said. "But she could be followed. She shouldn't be coming out here to see you. The Meekses are a crime family and they are all pretty upset with you."

"Mafia, right? I *knew* it," Margo said triumphantly.

"Yeah, well, maybe you see why you need to stay out of sight as well. When people are that mad, they'll hurt your loved ones, your friends . . . they've made an association now between you and Mr. Knox. They'll get payback for Julian's death any way they can. Now, the captain also agreed to put tails on the other two suspects."

"What other suspects?" Russell shouted, excited to have someone beside himself under suspicion.

"I'm not at liberty to say," Finn said, looking at Margo pointedly.

She knew exactly what two suspects he meant, but Russell really didn't need to think his brother had killed someone and tried to frame him until it could be proven beyond all doubt.

"Could I talk to you a sec?" Margo asked. She and Finn stepped out of the car.

"You are being way too paranoid. Nobody is out to get me. I've got a business to run. A medical check-up tomorrow. Oh, yeah, remember the heart transplant? This one's a big deal—I've got to take a whole bunch of tests. And I do not want to go into hiding. I don't want to act scared because I'm not scared. I can take care of myself."

"Maybe I'm the one that's scared," Finn conceded.

"Then how's this—as safe as we know and hope that Russell will be here, if someone were to go after him, wouldn't being in the same place as him put me in the line of fire?"

She had a point.

"I still don't want you back at your place. What about . . . my place?"

"Your place?"

"Yeah, it's small, but the bed's comfortable." He couldn't help a guilty grin.

"Aren't you the sly one."

"And I'm going to call the station and have a detail assigned to your movie house."

"A guard outside the theater?"

"Inside. Right next to the ticket booth."

"You're going to scare the customers."

"No uniform. Give him some Milk Duds and he'll just look like he's waitin' for someone. Just a few days. The Meekses won't be a problem if we can find Julian's killer."

What if it's Fiona? Margo wondered.

Anywhere but Finn's place and she might have objected to leaving her home. "I'll call Bette and tell her I'll be at your place for a while," she conceded, trying not to tip off that this was actually an exciting turn of events.

"I have an *Aliens* marathon all ready for you. Let's get Russell settled in. Call his fiancée. Pick up some clothes for you. And go over to my place and . . . take a nap."

"Fine."

"Super fine."

He could be such a goof. But they were both in need of a break from the unanswered questions and violent undertones of recent days.

*****

Their second "night" together cemented an attachment that was barreling past the point of no return. For two people who had spent their adult lives falling asleep with the certainty of early death casting a gloomy shadow over every sunrise, unmitigated joy had taken its place.

"Stay in bed. You've got a full shift tonight," Margo told him.

"If I don't drive you to the theater, I'm going to have Charlie stop by here and pick you up," Finn said, reaching for his phone. "He's got theater detail tonight."

"Mr. Milk Duds?"

"That's right. Throw the guy a bone. We'll have dinner tonight, right? Before I go in?"

Finn fell asleep holding Margo's hand. She reluctantly disentangled herself when her cellphone vibrated with Charlie's arrival.

The following twenty-four hours, Margo was enveloped in a bubble of safety, which she decided not to object to in the short run. Especially since the attempt on Russell's life seemed to have lit a fire under the police force. He was still their main suspect, but Finn was heavily pushing them to broaden the investigation.

If an innocent man were killed because they had pointed the finger at the wrong man—that was an unthinkable scenario.

Margo did have to make time to go to the hospital the following day. The results would be part of an official nationwide update on the aftermath of all transplants performed that year. She knew her results would be stellar, and she was happy for Dr. Svenson to get the credit for it. Good thing his colleagues would never know why her new heart was so unbelievably sturdy. The fact that it came from a witch actually wouldn't land him in as much legal hot water as the fact that there was no donor permission.

Margo was waiting by the nurse's station for the last of her tests, trying to keep Newhart entertained through the bars of his carrier. Then she glanced down the hallway and saw a heartwarming sight coming toward her. It was Rowena Quinn being pushed in a wheelchair, her tiny little baby wrapped in her arms.

"Oh, wow," Margo gushed. "It looks like everything went great. Can I take a look? At him? Her?"

"Her. A little girl. Just like I always wanted."

Margo peeked at the tiny head, already sprouting a thick patch of black hair.

"She's beautiful. What wonderful news for your whole family. Where is the proud daddy?"

"Oh, the doctor told us it was going to be a really long labor. And Lester really wasn't going to be any help in the labor room. He gets so queasy—you know how some guys are. So I told him to scram and wait for my call. And my sister came down from Boston to help me out. She's all the company I needed."

"Ah, well, congratulations to you all," Margo said sincerely.

The nurse at the station echoed the sentiment. "There's nothing I love more than seeing a healthy family go home. I've got the form for the birth certificate you filled out right here. We just need to print out the official copy."

Newhart chose that moment to show off his special trick of escaping his plush cage. He jumped to the floor, and with anther quick leap, landed right on the edge of the birth document, where he immediately hocked out a fur ball right onto the birth document.

"Oh, no. Newhart. That's awful. Oh, I'm so sorry."

"Ew." The nurse recoiled.

Margo reached over the counter for the box of tissues on the nurse's desk. She scooped up the fur ball and tried to wipe off the document as much as possible.

"No, no. Don't bother. We'll have to get a new form filled out. That's not going to go back into my file cabinet. Sorry, Mrs. Quinn. I'll be right back."

"Yeah. Sorry about that," Margo repeated guiltily. Of all things to ruin, a document testifying to the creation of a new life. Her tiny little family tree, laying out the legal particulars that established her place in the world. Parents. City of birth. Blood types . . . blood types.

"That's peculiar. The baby's blood type is B positive. Good motto. Easy to remember. Now, it's been a long time since my last biology class, but I'm pretty sure that means one of her parents has to also have B blood type. But you're O negative—universal, very nice. And your husband is type A.

And the two of you managed to create a B positive child. You know who else had B positive blood? Julian Meeks did. His brother mentioned that when I interviewed the family."

Rowena's face was frozen still—she looked like the classic deer in the headlights. This one was not too difficult to figure out.

"I imagine that your husband would be pretty angry to find out that this is his cousin Julian's child."

Rowena's face clouded over, as did her sister's. Their expressions spilled the beans.

"I see. He already knows," Margo continued. "And he already got really angry. Angry enough to kill his own cousin."

Rowena started stammering. "It was . . . it was all my fault. I– I should have stayed away from Julian. And we never should have tried to live in that big house together. Lester was always gone every night on business. Things just got out of hand."

"Shut up, Rowena," her sister snapped at her.

"It's too late. The truth is right there in the baby's blood," Rowena replied. Then she turned to Margo. "Of course, Lester was furious—what man wouldn't be? But he shouldn't be punished for something I drove him to do. It's just too much. The baby's father is dead. His brother is in prison for trying to kill that Russell guy. And my husband—he's all we got left. Our

166

family will be devastated. Destroyed. What's going to happen to this little baby?"

Margo was unmoved. "If she's lucky, you'll do everything you can to surround her with better people."

She left Rowena sobbing and her sister shaken.

Outside, Margo quickly called Finn on her cell. "Lester Quinn killed his cousin Julian Meeks. He found out that his wife and Julian were having an affair, and the baby that she just had is Julian's. I just saw her at the hospital. She admitted everything."

"What? She admitted everything? Where's Lester right now?"

"He's at his lumber office."

"Okay, hang on a minute. I gotta get on the other line, check the tap and the tracker we've got on his phone, and get some cops out there."

"You have a tracker on his phone? How did you know?"

"That he killed Julian? We didn't. He's been under investigation for a long time for Mafia stuff. But they were never able to pin anything on him. Hang on."

After a long five-minute wait, Finn was back on the line. "Yeah he's at his lumber business, right now . . . lumber. Wood rot. Arsenic. Yeah, it took a little too long to connect those dots. Anyway, I'm meeting most of the other officers over there for the arrest. But I don't want you at the hospital. His wife just had a baby. He could be headed over there. And it looks like they're putting everyone on this, so no one's left for guard duty."

"I could get over to your place," Margo volunteered.

"No. No people have seen us and I don't even want to risk them tracking down my place. His wife is going to give him a heads up for sure. He's going to know that you know. But no one can connect you to the hotel. I want you to join Russell. He's in room 208. Just wait it out. I checked on him just an hour ago. You two sit tight until Lester is brought in. Then I'll pick you up. Okay? You did terrific. Now, let the cops do their thing. Okay?"

"Okay."

Margo heard Finn's loud sigh of relief.

"Take a cab. There's always a few outside the hospital."

"Yeah, I see one."

Margo was quite willing to comply. Anyone who killed his own cousin wouldn't hesitate to kill Russell or herself. Thank goodness it was all about to be over.

*****

Margo exited the taxi. She stepped through a tall hedged fence toward the motel entrance. *Click.* She turned to find herself staring down along the barrel of a handgun, about twelve feet away, held by a cold, steely Lester Quinn.

"Not a very smart move, sticking your nose in our family business."

"Well, I didn't, really. It was just this hairball mishap," Margo said, mind racing, and stalling for time seemed like the first line of defense. "I wasn't thinking about your family at all. How could I even have imagined that a man would kill his own cousin?"

"Oh, yeah. Can you imagine a man's wife and cousin stabbing him in the back? Messing around, right under my own roof."

Margo took a closer look at the gun. Was that a silencer? "Oh, I'm sure it was very hurtful."

"It's not like it's a secret that can really be kept. The truth would have to come out. Julian would treat the kid like she was his own. The whole world would found out. The Quinns and Meeks would be laughingstocks. As it is, now I gotta raise someone else's kid and pretend it's mine. I don't think I'm gonna be able to stand the sight of this kid. But I gotta deal with it to keep the family together. Nothing more important than family."

"Family? You not only killed your cousin, but you pinned the blame on Russell, which made Julian's brother so upset he could wind up in prison for years."

"Carson would have saved me a lot of trouble if he could've been a little quicker with his car. Maybe just as well. I would have to watch my back and worry that Carson was going to find out I killed his brother. Now, he's in jail, and he can't get to me. But that did leave me the little problem of taking care you and Russell Knox by myself."

"How did you even know we were here?" Margo asked, knowing it didn't matter since Lester seemed pretty intent on killing her.

"Oh, guess it don't matter if I tell you. We got ourselves a couple of inside men on the police force, one in Boston and one here in Oyster Cove. Barney Thomas, Rowena's cousin. Tells us everything we need to know. What motel you were being stashed in. How the cops been tracking my phone, which I left over in the lumber office for them. By the time they get over here, you'll both be dead, and Russell will have typed a confession on his computer about killing Julian and then killing you when you confronted him with the murder, and then deciding he couldn't live with what he had done. Brilliant, right?"

Oh, how Lilith wished she were facing this man in Margo's place. He was just the sort of slimy lowlife that she used to take such pleasure in disposing of. But more to the point, it looked as if Margo's life was about to be extinguished. Along with the hope of any possibility of her assistance in finding Lilith's killer.

Now, the questions in Margo's mind began swirling in earnest. Was she finally face-to-face with the abrupt death that had threatened her for her entire life? Was she going to turn into a ghost? Would she be able to see Lilith and talk to her? What would it do to Finn to find her dead? That question snapped her back into survival mode.

If only Lester were close enough, she would send a jolt of electricity through him that he would not soon forget. But he was too far away. She had to be close enough to touch him, and if she made a lunge for him . . . well, she was most certainly not faster than a speeding bullet.

And Lester knew his way around the gun. He had both hands gripping it and it appeared to be aimed right at her heart. What a despicable man—no qualms about killing innocent people. Just a quick tug on the trigger, and her life would disappear into nothing and he would just blithely make his way up to Russell's room and do it all over again. If only his gun turned out to be defective in some way or . . . or broken.

"*Refractere!*" Margo roared, one hand outstretched toward the gun, the other on her pendant.

Lester let out a scream of extreme pain and dropped the gun on the ground. A split-second later, Finn came out of nowhere and tackled Lester to the ground. Lester continued screaming.

"My hands! My hands are broken!"

"Stay down and shut up," Finn ordered.

He put handcuffs on Lester, which made him scream even louder.

"What do you know? His hands *are* broken. Could've sworn he landed on his shoulder. But buddy, you just had that gun pointed at my girl. So I don't care if you have fifty-seven bones broken. Babe, you okay?"

"I am now," Margo said.

Finn called in for backup. He and Margo held each other close while they waited for the cops and ambulance to arrive.

"How did you know that he was coming here?" Margo asked.

"I didn't. But there were so many guys headed out to the bust at the lumber company that I decided that I needed to . . . I told the captain I had to see how you were doing."

"Never better." Margo rested her head against his chest. They rested in a silent embrace. Well, silent except for Lester's crying and whining.

"I'll probably get charged with excessive force. I still don't know how the guy's hands got broken. But I could care less. When I think about what could've happened . . ."

"Don't worry about his hands. Twenty minutes and they'll be good as new. Not that he deserves it."

Finn was puzzled, but Margo had been through so much, it was no surprise that she wasn't thinking clearly.

"Oh, and there's this guy on the force, Barney Thomas. He's Rowena's cousin, and he's been feeding the family information about which motel was the safe house and how Lester's phone was being traced. This is probably why you were never able to get any information from the Mafia investigation. And they've got another family guy in the Boston force as well."

"Barney Thomas. Never liked him."

By the time the cop cars and ambulance arrived, there was such a commotion happening outside the motel that it drew Russell out of hiding. He approached Finn and Margo cautiously.

"Russell!" Margo ran over and gave him a big hug "It's over. We're safe now. And Julian Meeks's killer is headed for jail."

Russell was speechless. Almost. "Margo, you've saved my life. You really have."

What a weight was finally lifted from Margo's shoulders. She was finally forgiven. Not by Russell . . . but by herself.

*****

Fortunately, the arrest of Lester Quinn occurred on a Monday, Margo's only day off from the theater. Which was lucky timing. She had a lot to process and would not have been very focused on chatting about movie trivia or reviews with her talkative customers.

Everything had worked out, perhaps not neatly, but with some justice. There would be some difficult days ahead for Russell in reestablishing his business. But perhaps, with one loan shark dead and two others in prison, at least his loan was history.

A knock on the door had her racing to the entrance, and a moment later, she wrapped her arms around Finn, who looked absolutely exhausted from his very long day at the office.

"C'mere. We need to talk," Finn said.

They sat down on the sofa and Margo waited expectantly.

"Something very strange happened with Lester Quinn. You saw how his hands were broken. Which is just a bizarre injury, for starters. Then, we get him over to the hospital, and the doctor gets around to him. By then, he had stopped hollering. And no wonder—his hands weren't broken anymore. You hear what I'm saying? The hands that were broken were no longer broken. And immediately, I remembered something bizarre you had said. That in twenty minutes, his hands would be fine. Which was ridiculous. Except . . . it turned out to be true."

Margo drew in a deep breath. Was Finn going to be able to handle this? Would it change things between them?

"I do have something to tell you."

"I'm all ears."

"You're not from Oyster Cove. You probably don't know a whole lot about witches."

"Witches! All I know about witches is that there's nothing to know. The fellas at the precinct are always 'witch this, witch that'. This is the most superstitious town I've ever been in. You tellin' me you believe in that kind of thing?"

Margo scooted over on the sofa closer to him and gently touched the sleeve of his white shirt. "*Resplenda.*"

The shirt changed into a beautiful sea green. Finn drew in a quick breath and leaned back a few inches, eyes darting back and forth between Margo and the shirt.

"Yeah, I didn't know much about witches either," Margo said gently. "Until my heart transplant."

Finn's face was, by turns, quite expressive and then eerily calm as Margo detailed the development of her witchly powers. Throughout her talk, whenever a wave of disbelief came over his features, she reached over and did another quick color-change on him to purple, orange, and electric blue. Each time was effective in overriding his natural skepticism.

As she concluded, Margo tried to assess his reaction. "I was a little worried you would freak out. But you're not freaking out."

"Oh, yes, I am. I'm a trained operative. This is what we look like when we're freaking out."

"No rush. It's a lot to take in. I should probably have mentioned that this is something you have to keep on the down low. You can't tell anyone."

"And have them think I'm a nutcase? You'd better believe this is something I can keep to myself." He shook his head, needing one final bit of evidence. He pointed toward a vase on the coffee table. "Break that vase."

"*Refractere.*"

The vase shattered. Finn settled back on the sofa in deep thought.

"Franc for your thoughts?" Margo inquired warily.

"If I could taser people and break equipment, I wouldn't have nearly as many bullet holes in me."

"You're jealous!"

"You've got some serious skills."

"Oh, I'm just getting started. There's so much more to learn."

"What's the most extreme thing you've done?"

"Well, at the cliff dive . . . that actually was a shark."

"Oh, man!"

This was going better than Margo had anticipated. Then she became worried again when she found herself under close, quiet scrutiny.

"And you say it changed you. That you're stronger . . . bolder . . . different?"

"I am different. I just can't say for sure how much of the differences are coming from Lilith, or whether I'm turning into the Margo I would have been if I had been born with a healthy heart. I do know one thing—Lilith Hazelwood was an extraordinary person, but she didn't have a lot of love in her." Margo pressed the back of her hand against Finn's heart. "That part's all me."

Finn drew Margo closer. Funny how a revelation as remarkable as witchcraft could quickly be bumped from center stage.

CHAPTER FOURTEEN: EPILOGUE

F inn and the police captain were happy to do Russell the favor of going to the hospital and delivering the message of Russell's innocence directly to his grandfather. Later that same afternoon, the will was revised yet again, and Russell was set to receive his inheritance. Three days later, during a lucid moment, his grandfather requested an end to the life-support. It gave Russell tremendous peace of mind to be able to hold his grandfather's hands for that final moment.

*****

It did take a few weeks for Russell's restaurant to lure the customers back. Margo did everything in her power to assist. Fortunately, she had a lot of power to draw on. She went to Ian Fowler to demand some assistance. After all, he'd played a big part in Russell's misfortunes.

"All's fair in love and war," Ian sneered. "Bad enough the guy's back. Don't know why I would be giving him a hand."

"Are you forgetting how you messed up his liquor license? Took away his first six months of profits? It's time to make up for all of that."

"And just what did you have in mind?"

"The restaurant next to me and I have this deal where we arrange discounts together for customers. You and Russell could do some advertising and discounting together, sending customers each other's way."

"Forget about it. Survival of the fittest, that's what I always say."

"Hope you have a good supply of candles," Margo said pointedly.

Ian shrugged his shoulders in confusion. "Now, if you'll excuse me . . ."

There was no quantity of candles that could have handled Ian's upcoming electricity crisis. His restaurant lost power that night, and despite the best efforts of one team of electricians after another, no one could locate the problem. He was shut down for two weeks while they tried.

In the meantime, hungry customers who came for *Verona* were just as happy to cross the street and nibble on the goodies on offer in *Barcelona*. During the two weeks that Ian's restaurant was out of commission, Russell's restaurant filled again to capacity.

*****

One of the first Monday evenings, however, the restaurant was closed for a private party. There was so much to celebrate. Russell's freedom. A big thank-you to Margo and Finn for everything they had done. And a bon voyage party for Bette.

"Bon appétit," Bette said giddily. She couldn't believe that she was finally going to see Paris.

"How much did you say those tickets were?" Wendy asked.

"Four fifty round-trip, Boston to Paris. I know, it's crazy good. I think they had a big group cancellation and only one week to fill up the seats. It's gonna be nice to stay in a hotel for once and not be the one running the hotel. And I have an old friend from high school who is working there now. She can show me around. I can't wait!"

Margo beamed. No longer was the need to babysit her sick heart going to hold Bette back from seeing the world.

"I want to see Paris," Finn's cousin, Zoe, said wistfully.

"I'll scope out all the good spots for you," Bette promised.

"Take a walk through Montmartre," Dr. Svenson recommended. "That was my favorite."

"And be sure to take a boat ride on the Seine at night," Delphine recommended. "It's magical."

Naughty Delphine. She and Margo exchanged a smile. Russell raised a glass of wine and the others joined him.

"To a wonderful voyage for Bette. And to Margo, who will have my eternal gratitude for as long as I live, as well as all the free tapas she can eat."

Everyone cheered. Finn squeezed Margo's hand. This boisterous communal celebration was a fitting prelude for their new life ahead.

*****

Russell's brother, Walter, ended up selling his house, which had enough equity in it to restore his clients' accounts and get the credit cards off his back. Delphine and Margo crossed paths on the boardwalk early one afternoon, and Margo was reminded that there was a question she had wanted to ask Delphine for some time.

"You gave an enormous amount of cash to Walter Knox right outside your shop," Margo said. "It's none of my business, but okay, what gives?"

"Oh, Walter? Dear, he's kind of a dope. But I kept running into him every time I went to Atlantic City. Specifically, at the baccarat table at the Borgata."

Margo was quite surprised. "You're a gambler?"

"The thing is . . .when you can control and change and manipulate as much as we can, you don't get to experience the thrill of good luck or the absolutely insufferable bad luck that makes you want to strangle someone." She chuckled. "It's sort of a little challenge for me, accepting what comes and holding back the urge to twist it to my advantage. Kind of like when commoners go roughing it out in the woods, but with comped beverages."

"You're full of surprises."

"So I saw Walter all the time. He's got a big mouth. He got himself banned from a lot of casinos in town. And the Borgata is not the place you want to be banned from. But he messed up. So now, when he knows I'm going, he gives me his cash and says to spend it alongside my money. If it loses, it loses. Whatever it wins, I bring it back to him. Like I said, he's kind of a schmo, but why not?"

"How often do you go?" Margo asked.

"Gambling is fun, but the truth is . . . my fella is a maître d' at the Borgata. I've gone down every couple of weeks for the past fifteen years, and we have a good time together. I just started hanging out at of the game tables to kill time while he was working."

Margo wasn't sure why she was so pleased. Delphine had a boyfriend! "What's he like? Okay, who would play him? Living or dead."

Delphine cocked her head. "Anthony Quinn."

"Ooh. Zorba."

They both laughed.

"Does he know?" Margo wondered.

"Absolutely not. He's not a young man. No need to give him a heart attack. A witch's life is always going to have its fair share of secrets."

At that moment, Delphine spotted Fiona down the street. That woman was a whole encyclopedia of secrets, one of which she had just revealed to Delphine the other day. And just as she brazenly paraded her powers in front of commoners, she was more than happy to let Delphine know that her family had triumphed over Lilith Hazelwood's.

"Lilith had quite a vengeful nature. I'm not sure what she would have done if she found out that my mother had killed hers. Oh, yes. Those two had quite a rivalry, but my mother was the stronger of the two by far," Fiona boasted.

"And what was the offense?" Delphine had inquired.

"The Hazelwoods' affronts are too numerous to count. The important thing is that, even though she didn't get a chance to know her mother, knowing how she was ended could very well have turned Lilith's wrath in my direction. I certainly can't cry tears over her . . . misfortune. Better her than me."

It was not exactly an admission of guilt. It could simply be that Fiona was quite fond of intimidating others with her family's mastery of the dark arts. But of all the witches in town, Fiona was uniquely capable, and now uniquely motivated, to have sent Lilith to her grave. Could she have murdered the stronger witch preemptively? Thankfully, Delphine had not felt Lilith's presence during this revelation. She would have jumped to conclusions that could still not be substantiated.

Delphine certainly didn't want to trouble Margo with this news. With no daughters of her own, she had developed quite an attachment to the new young witch. She would hate to see her suffer from the worst impulses of either Fiona or Lilith. Especially at this moment in life, when it was such a pleasure to see her so happy.

*****

Margo stepped breezily out of the local DMV, new driver's license in hand.

"Newhart."

From his hiding spot in the nearby bushes, Newhart ran out immediately. He had graduated from his cage, having developed a high level of reliability and attachment. He would pad softly after Margo when she was out and about, and he never wandered too far out of earshot.

"Okay. We're going to wait here for Finn and go get some breakfast. Maybe a little lox for you?"

Did Newhart lick his lips? He really seemed to be getting smarter by the day.

Margo looked down at her newly minted license. It was a decent photo, even downright flattering. But what gave her the greatest satisfaction was being able to fill in the organ donor box.

Not that she believed that she would meet with an untimely end and that the donation would actually come into effect. Like a fortuneteller, her heart whispered to her every night that she would live a long and happy life.

But after it had served two full lifetimes, there was a real possibility that Lilith's heart might still be vital. In which case, she would be happy to know that someone like herself would get it. Improbable, but what about her recent life had been 'probable'?

"My dear Margo, how good to see you," Dr. Svenson boomed behind her. "Thank you for inviting me to such a special occasion. I enjoyed your friends very much."

"They loved meeting you too," Margo assured him.

That was putting it mildly. The doctor who saved Margo's life was treated like a rock star.

"Your young man is very nice."

"I know."

"You lost your father at a very early age—before you knew him, yes? These past several years, I wasn't sure whether we were going to be able to get you a heart—whether you were going to make it. And I always prayed that you would live longer than me, fall in love, get married, and that I would have the honor of escorting you down the aisle. A doctor's dreams are probably not what you imagined, eh?"

Margo threw her arms around the doctor.

"I would love that. I never thought I'd have anyone for that."

"What's this? What's this? Come on, Doc, get your mitts off my girl," Finn said behind them.

"I'm too busy for a duel right now. She's all yours," Dr. Svenson said, backing away with a smile. "Check-up in two weeks, young lady."

"I'll pass with flying colors," Margo replied with supreme confidence.

"I know you will. I just like for you to visit."

Before he turned and walked away, he pointed at Finn behind his back and gestured at him hopefully. Margo wagged a warning finger at him. For heaven's sake. It was too soon to be thinking about marriage. Too soon to be talking, too soon to be thinking. Oh, who was she kidding? Of course, the thought had crossed her mind, maybe even more than a couple of times. The nice thing was, Finn had made it clear that the thought was crossing his mind too.

"Tonight's the big night. I'm prepared for another transformative experience," Finn said.

"I hope you're taking this very seriously. This is the defining movie experience for the entire Bailey family. If it weren't for this movie, my name could be . . . Bertha."

They chuckled and joined hands as they strolled down the street.

"*All about Eve*, eh? I know for a fact that this Margo is not going to hold a candle to my Margo, but I'll try to give her a chance."

Ooh, take that, Margo Channing. "I guess I'll be fine if she becomes your second favorite Margo. Hey, Newhart. Stop playing with that dog. She does not want to play with you." Newhart was circling a tiny dog who was cowering nervously.

Finn chimed in. "Yeah, Newhart. Get over here. Newhart. New . . . Hart. Wait a minute. New . . . Heart. New heart." Finn looked at Margo a bit sheepishly. "I just got it. Why are you laughing? How should I know? You like old actors. I thought you might be a big Bob Newhart fan."

Still laughing, Margo scooped Newhart up and started running down the street, Finn sprinting behind her.

Lilith shook her head in exasperation. It was still difficult to say whether Margo Bailey was going to be of any use to her. On the one hand, she entered potentially dangerous confrontations without hesitation. She faced down a killer and kept her wits about her. Her powers were rudimentary, but growing. On the other hand . . . what an inconvenient time for her to fall in love, a distraction that Lilith had never succumbed to. It would blunt Margo's capacity for anger and complicate using her as an instrument of vengeance.

Lilith would have to assess all of her options before she knew for sure. She cast an eye on the disappearing figure of Dr. Svenson and swiftly made her way to his side. Loathsome man, taking her apart like that. The spectacle of a multitude of her body parts being placed into their new hosts was a sight that would be seared into her eternal memory.

Now, the doctor would lead her to the other recipients, one of whom might display exceptional talent and utility. One who could solve the murder of Lilith Hazelwood and grant her the sweet justice she deserved.